Runaway

Runaway

A COLLECTION OF STORIES

Mary Clearman Blew

Short
Fiction
Series

Confluence Press

A James R. Hepworth Book

Acknowledgements

Grateful acknowledgement is made to the editors of the following magazines in which many of these stories first appeared:

Ball State Literary Forum, "College Bound 1957;"
Four Quarters, "Alberta's Story," "Last Night As I Lay on the Prairie" (as "Endings"), "A Lesson in Hunter Safety," "The Snowies, the Judiths," "Stall Warning;"
The Georgia Review, "Album" (as "Paths Unto the Dead," which also appeared in *Best American Short Stories 1974*), "Forby and the Mayan Maidens" (which also appeared in *Necessary Fictions: Selected Stories from the Georgia Review*), "Granddaughters," "Samples's Crossing;"
The North American Review, "I Beat the Midget;"
Scratchgravel Hills, "Bare Trees."

Special thanks are offered to James R. Hepworth and Tanya Gonzales for their friendship and criticism, to Andrew Caldwell for his assistance in preparing this manuscript for publication, and to Penney Bergren for her love and perseverance.

ISBN 0-917652-77-0
LIBRARY OF CONGRESS CARD NUMBER 88-062764

Publication of this book is made possible by grants from the Idaho Commission on the Arts, a State agency, and the National Endowment for the Arts in Washington, D.C., a Federal agency.

Cover design: Karla Fromm

Production and Design by Tanya Gonzales with assistance from Judi Lanphier and Juan Martinez

Published by

Distributed to the trade by

Confluence Press, Inc.
Lewis Clark State College
8th Avenue & 6th Street
Lewiston, Idaho 83501

National Book Network
4720-A Boston Way
Lanham, Maryland 20706

for Rachel

Contents

College Bound
1957

On her way to the session on secondary teacher education, Margaret got caught for running and was sent to the counselor's office for a pink slip and therefore burst into the physics lab late to find a small gray-haired man in a gray suit standing in front of the sink and explaining to thirty high school seniors that, in a rural state, most ed majors ended up teaching in very small high schools, so they might as well accept the fact from the beginning.

He stopped and watched Margaret find an empty desk and stuff her skirts under it. Everybody in the lab turned and watched, too. All the town girls had started wearing layers of stiff crinolines under their full skirts the previous spring, and Margaret and her younger sister tried to dress just like them. When their father brought them to school in the truck, their crinolines nearly crowded him out of the cab.

"To get a job in a small high school, you need to be flexible," the gray-haired man went on, with a final glance at Margaret to make sure she felt too conspicuous to move. "I always advise my secondary ed majors at Eastern to pick up plenty of minors. What are you going to minor in?"

A strange girl by the window, one of the students bused in for the day from a country high school, raised her hand. "Driver's ed and typing?" she ventured.

Everybody grinned, because she wore a fringed coat like an Indian jacket that none of them would have been caught dead in, but the gray-haired man cried, "Driver's ed and typing! That's what I like to hear!"

Nancy Stevens, whom Margaret knew from fourth-year algebra class, raised her hand. "I want to teach in college," she said. "What should I take?"

The gray-haired man snorted at her. "You have to teach in high

3

school a good many years before any college dean will look at you! You might as well take the same program as everybody else."

He went on to explain about rural school superintendents and how they liked to see a good solid average college record. "When I was a superintendent, I wouldn't hire somebody with straight A's. If I saw straight A's on a transcript, I wouldn't give him a second look."

Nancy Stevens twitched. She had straight A's.

Margaret yawned and half-listened. She had long known enough to keep her subversive thoughts to herself. But when silence fell, she raised her hand. "Theater arts and physics?" she suggested.

And the gray-haired man nodded, slowly, his eyes growing thoughtful as he studied her: Was she being a smart aleck or not?

"If you can just get enough schooling so they'll let you teach, that's the main thing. When I started normal school, Ma wanted me to stay for the full two years, but I found out I could get my teaching certificate in five quarters, and I didn't see the sense in wasting any more of her money."

Margaret made no reply. Her mother's voice wound on, complaining, reciting her litany of her own mother's errors, but the sound and sense faded from Margaret's ears. Margaret's speculations were decorated with more vivid stuff, and her thoughts roved through intricate convolutions while her body, in a ragged wool overcoat and her father's old gloves, moved through the routine of her chores: laying feed in every stanchion, turning on the pressure in the milking system, shoving open the double barn doors.

Once outside the barn, the bitter air woke her to sharp reality. The afternoon was gone. Flakes of snow fell through the electric light on the pole above the barn and vanished into a corral full of jangling cowbells. The dairy herd, thirty black-and-white Holsteins and six raw-boned Brown Swiss, butted at each other and trampled over the frozen mud and manure. Each cow held her own ground, and the others fought her if she stepped out of it. When Margaret swung open the gate, they lumbered past her in single file in their predetermined order, huge udders swaying and eyes bulging at the smell of grain in their troughs. Margaret, trapped in the present by the odor of warm milk in the freezing air and the sudden stench of hot green liquefaction pouring from under an upraised tail, followed the last cow into the barn and began to lock stanchions around necks lowered to their feed.

She was remembering how the gray-haired man from Eastern Montana College had told them there was no such thing as a two-year teaching certificate any more. If they wanted to teach, it was the full four-year program for them. She thought of telling her mother what he had said, but her mother already had gone back to the springhouse to start the coolers.

Margaret's thoughts slipped back into the splendid passages of her imagination while her hands took up the wire hook. She tossed the end of a short rope around the hocks of the Brown Swiss that kicked, used the hook to snare the loop end of the rope, drew it snug, and unseeingly snubbed it to a post. Her sister Karen, wrapped in her own thoughts, came up with a bucket of warm water and began to wash mud and crusted green manure off the massive udder.

Margaret turned on the suction and staggered back to the cow with a surcingle over her shoulder and a fifty-pound Surge milker banging against her leg. She hung the surcingle over the cow's back and buckled it and suspended the milking machine under her belly. Then she knelt and carefully fitted each teat, one by one, into a suction cup with a little *suck* while the cow shifted her weight uneasily and worked her leg against the rope. Margaret sat back on her heels and watched to see that the machine was chug-chugging on its own with no leak of air or pinched teat in the suction cup. Then she got up and lugged the second milker after her sister to the next cow.

Between them, with three Surge machines, Margaret and Karen could milk thirty-six cows in an hour and a half, and they could do it in silence, through a haze, out of their two separate realms. Margaret's body went through the motions, emptying milkers into pails, avoiding the constant *splat-splat* of reeking excreta from one cow or another, but before her eyes were brilliant lights and bright colors, shifting into farther and farther corridors through which she, the star, wandered at will.

On Monday Margaret stopped by the high school counselor's office to read the scholarship offers on his bulletin board. Mr. Halloran was teaching his junior history class at that hour, so Margaret leaned against the wainscoting and watched the winter light fall on the clutter of pamphlets and bulletins and spun the threads of a dream about winning an all-expense-paid scholarship to Pasadena Playhouse.

Mr. Halloran walked in and dumped his briefcase on a table already deep in college brochures. "Still at it, are you?" he remarked.

"I was thinking about this Eddy's Bread Scholarship," said Margaret.

Mr. Halloran glanced at the poster and groaned. "You want to go to the trouble of an application for a measly twenty-five dollar scholarship?"

"Twenty-five dollars is twenty-five dollars," said Margaret, puzzled.

"What's it going to take to get through to you, Margaret?"

She stared at him, wondering what he meant. He was a large man with pale hair combed straight back from his face. Ten years ago he had been a basketball star for the state university. Now he terrorized the smaller high school fry with his sarcasm and his sheer bulk.

"I've asked your parents to come talk to me," he said.

"Why?"

He stood up from the corner of his desk and glared down at her. "Because I can't get through to you! What's the matter with you? Was it the part in the play that went to your head?"

She kept her eyes down in case he could read her mind, but he gave a snort of exasperation. "Go on, get out of here! Go to class!"

The bell had just rung. Students with armloads of books poured out of classroom doors and jostled in the halls, jabbering at the tops of their voices for the few minutes between classes. Caught like a twig in their current, Margaret was swept away from the counselor's door, along the corridor, and washed up at last, alone, in the alcove by the gym. High and dry and unnoticed, she looked down the stairs at the knots of exclusive girls, bright and loud as parrots in their skirts and sweaters. And the groups of boys—the cowboys, the stars, the hoods—bound by indefinable threads, staking their territorial claims to the stairs, the landing, the drinking fountain.

Margaret felt a sinking sensation. For a breath she knew what it was to be nobody, a shell—not even Margaret with her big feet, Margaret with her muscles, Margaret the all-too-plausible butt of jokes—only an empty thing, an observer, never a participant.

She shut her eyes. Gradually sound and sense faded, and she gathered the threads of her dream around her again.

The idea of Mount Holyoke had come to her a year ago, when two boys in the class ahead of her had won scholarships to Dartmouth, and Stephanie Zann, whose math she had been doing for two years, remarked that all those eastern colleges would bend over backwards to get students from the West. She and Stephanie had gone to get application blanks from Mr. Halloran, and Mr. Halloran had hit the ceiling.

"Do you have the faintest idea what you'd be getting into?" he kept asking Margaret, and she didn't know how to answer him.

He called her parents, who were nearly as alarmed as he was. "How do you get these ideas in your *head?*" her mother kept asking, as suspicious as if she thought Margaret's head was a ragbag of crazy ideas. Margaret herself began to feel the precarious balance of her head on the stem of her neck.

Her father told how he had got to talking with one of the county commissioners, who said *his* daughter had gone to the state university and made lifelong friends there, which was something you couldn't do in an out-of-state college. *He* hadn't lost anything out of state, the county commissioner had said. Montana was good enough for him.

Her mother had heard that, at out-of-state schools, all the students were snobs. A woman she knew had a friend whose

7

daughter had gone back East to college and reported that all the other girls had fur coats—"And there I was in my little cloth coat!"

For a week Margaret's parents worried about little else, but in the end Mr. Halloran solved their problem by simply not sending in Margaret's scholarship application.

Stephanie Zann's application went in, but Stephanie, as it turned out, wasn't accepted, which in an odd way reconciled Margaret to never having applied at all. Eventually she stopped talking about Mount Holyoke. By that time she had read about Pasadena Playhouse.

So she had lost out on Mount Holyoke, but she never had expected any difficulties in getting to the state university. Certain of her plans, she had had the wisdom this time to keep them to herself. The bulletin from Pasadena Playhouse, advising a year's prior study at a good university, she also kept secret, knowing the least she could expect was ridicule. But she never had dreamed Mr. Halloran might seriously oppose her going to the state university.

But did he oppose her? Really?—it was so hard to be certain, so hard to know what was real and what was only in her head. A word, a sneer, the grin rising on his moon of a face—but Mr. Halloran was sarcastic to everybody, Margaret knew. Nothing to take personally, just his idea of humor. Besides, it was Mr. Halloran's job to see the seniors got into the colleges of their choice. The principal had said so, last September before the full assembly. What were her own perceptions, measured against such authority?—"Oh, Margaret, it's all in your *head!*" rang the aggrieved chorus from her teachers, her mother, her aunts, sometimes even her sister.

The bell was ringing; she was late for class again. Wrapping her arms around her load of library books, she hunched her head down and ran for it, between the stragglers, the hand-in-hand couples dawdling by the water fountain, the student council officers with their hall passes. Hardly anyone noticed Margaret, even when she bumped into them. She was a rift in their stream, a brief aberration, an invisible impediment; but she kept her eye on where she was going and reached the door of the physics lab just as the buzzer died.

"I can't see where it'll be so much cheaper for her to go to Eastern," her mother argued.

"It's a lot closer to home," said her father.

Margaret, washing buckets in the springhouse sink, saw their reflections in the dark window. Normally she would have submerged herself in her own thoughts and drowned out their quarrel, but tonight she listened like a spy while the water cooled on her hands.

"You can't count on her coming home on weekends to help out."

"Did I say I was?" shouted her father. "Did you hear me say I expected her to?"

It made it easy to spy when her parents, used to her daydreaming, assumed she heard only what was addressed directly to her. They went on talking as though she were a post or a stone, and Margaret listened while she slowly rinsed the last pail.

"Ev Halloran says he has to be fair to all the kids," her father explained, more reasonably. "If there's a spot for her at teacher's college, why should she take up somebody else's spot at the university?"

Her mother was stacking boxes of milk strainers. "Ma says a girl needs to be able to support herself same as a boy," she muttered.

Her father slammed down a bucket of separator parts on the concrete floor. "I never said she didn't!" he bellowed. "And neither did Ev Halloran! Ev's just looking at the kind of girl Margaret is, and where she'll be better off."

They finished washing up in angry silence. Margaret's mother turned off the light in the springhouse and hooked the door behind them. It was ten degrees below zero and getting colder as the wind blew the clouds off the stars.

"Ma says she'll help," she said.

Her father stiffened, and Margaret spared a tentacle from her scattered thoughts to explore the rough edges and contradictions in her mother's feelings for her grandmother.

"Anyway, it's only for two years," said her father.

Each high school in Montana could nominate up to three seniors to take the scholarship exam for the university. Stephanie Zann had it figured out. Last year's boys had nabbed all the spots, but this year's boys all wanted to work in filling stations and pay for their cars after graduation, so it looked automatic for Stephanie, Margaret, and Nancy Stevens. Margaret could hardly believe her ears when Mr. Halloran said no.

"Why?" she insisted.

"You shouldn't have to ask why."

"But *why?*"

Mr. Halloran rocked on the corner of his desk and regarded her with his pale eyes. Then he dropped an eyelid at her. "Oh, come on, Margaret. Do you really want to go clear to the U and leave Bill Anderson home?"

Margaret sat stupefied. Bill Anderson was one of the back-row boys. He had worked for her father last summer, haying. Apparently Mr. Halloran thought—maybe other people thought—and there came over her a creeping embarrassment, an awful surmise. This was what Mr. Halloran meant when he had told her parents, freshman year, that Margaret had a little social problem. Tears welled.

Mr. Halloran threw down his pen at the sight. "Oh, for God's sake! What have you got to cry about? Who do you think you are? Don't you realize what you're asking your parents to do?"

His normally bland face was so dark and contorted that Margaret stopped crying in astonishment. What could possibly be making Mr. Halloran so angry? She felt as though she had strayed across familiar ground and found a treacherous crust under her feet that cracked and boiled and threatened to disintegrate under her.

"Do you realize what they've gone through with that dairy? Do you want to ruin it all for them?"

"My grandmother said she'd help—"

"I want you to think about what you owe them, and settle

down! Eastern's a perfectly good school where you'll fit in if you'll just open your eyes and look at the world as it is!"

He paused and considered her, shaking his head. "You don't have any idea what you'd run up against at the U," he said, almost kindly.

"But—"

He threw up his hands. "Get out of here! Go to class!"

And Margaret slunk out, too amazed to shed more tears until much later. Why? Why? (It was a question, along with Mr. Halloran's *Who do you think you are?* that was to occupy her, off and on, for another thirty years.) Over and over, always to the same conclusion: Mr. Halloran was a counselor. Counselors had the best interests of their students at heart and would do what they could to get them into the colleges of their choice. Therefore—and at this point in Margaret's reasoning, her vision darkened and her ears roared with fear—Mr. Halloran must think she was not cut out for college.

Almost, she jumped off her stool and ran down the hall to ask him if this were so, but the thought of his sarcastic bark of laughter—"Well! You finally woke up to it, did you?"—froze her in the physics lab.

But—was it possible, could it be, that no one had had the heart to tell her what she should have known for herself? Had all her teachers known from the beginning that she belonged in the back row with boys like Bill Anderson?

She walked through the next weeks in gloom. In government class she watched Mr. Halloran and wondered if he stopped grinning in his sleep. He was surer of himself than anyone she knew. He was so big he scared the boys, and he had a knack for singling out and embarrassing any girl who had not read the assignment or didn't listen. Margaret was the only one he never had caught. Four years in his classes had taught her how to listen with one ear while she daydreamed so that, if he called on her, she could parrot back whatever he had been saying for the past ten minutes.

This dissociative ability, which had afforded her so many hours of imaginary splendor in the past, now gave her ample time for despair. All had fallen into place. At last she was seeing herself as she really was. Big Margaret. Big country Margaret, thinking she could step out of her mucky shoes into the golden circle when every sign, every omen, should have told her where she belonged. Had she ever once been invited to one of the senior parties? Had she been tapped for the senior honor society, many of whose members had lower grades than hers?

And so on until the Wednesday when the scholarship exams actually arrived from the university.

When she stopped at her locker after school, she saw Stephanie and Nancy, full of suppressed excitement, on their way to the counselor's office to take their exams. Margaret hauled on her coat and walked by herself to the main doors to wait for the school bus.

There had been a thaw, and the snow had melted into a muddy current that ran down the gutters in front of the high school and trickled through the stained crusts of ice. Leaning against the brick wall and watching the muddy stream were her sister Karen and the two Finstead girls, who lived so far out in the country they didn't know enough to carry their lunches in brown paper bags instead of black metal lunch pails. They were used to Margaret and hardly looked up as she settled herself against the wall to wait.

The double doors shot open. Stephanie, wild-eyed, burst out and caught Margaret by the arm.

"They sent all three exams by mistake! I asked the secretary if you could take the extra one, since it was here anyway, and she said it didn't matter to her!"

The bus pulled up, splashing muddy water across the sidewalk. Karen and the Finstead girls lined up.

"Come *on!*" urged Stephanie.

Karen turned and stared at her sister as if she never had seen her before.

"You'll miss the *bus!*" she said.

"I don't care."

"Who's going to *milk?*"

Margaret hesitated. Her sister's round blank eyes met hers. For the first time Margaret, whose rich daydreams had occupied her for years, wondered what took place in her sister's head.

"Mr. Halloran has it in for me!" she blurted.

"It's all in your *head!*" Karen shouted.

"I don't care!" Margaret shouted back.

Turning her back on the bus and Karen and the stolid Finsteads, she ran after Stephanie through the deserted halls and up the long flight of stairs to the counselor's office.

"—and I didn't know *what* I was going to do at the U without you to help me with my math—"

Mr. Halloran had gone to watch varsity basketball practice, as he did every afternoon, and the secretary, Mrs. Trepp, was proctoring the exams. She barely glanced at Margaret, just handed her a copy of the text booklet and told her to put her own books under the table.

Still wearing her coat, Margaret dropped into a chair and read the test instructions while she caught her breath. The thought of the cows waiting to be milked—and who would milk tonight?—Karen?—by herself?—warred with the overriding question: Was she, Margaret, cut out for college?

Then she read the first question, and all else faded. She liked taking exams. She was better at exams than anyone she knew. She began to mark her answers with the black IBM pencil.

"I learned today," said Mr. Halloran, "that one senior has won a university honor scholarship."

He looked across the clutter of the desk—the unopened mail, the photographs of his wife and look-alike blond children in a row—at Margaret. His pale eyes were expressionless.

"Didn't Stephanie get one?" Margaret blurted.

"No," he said. "No, she didn't." He looked down at his gnarled white basketball-playing fingers and then, not at Margaret, but beyond her. "I just want you to know," he said, "that I wash my hands of you."

Margaret sat like a lump in her chair, wondering what he meant, and then, following an irrelevant thread of curiosity, what about him was so changed. His big shoulders, rounded now from ten years behind a desk, his blunt thrusting head with its pale crest of hair, his pale eyes looking past her, searching for the door, for a way out—the grin. The grin was gone.

Out of her dense astonishment, the question surfaced: Why? (And rose again, on and off, through the years.) Why?

But at the time, she only knew she had won something and, in winning, had set her feet on ground that never would be certain again.

She overplayed her hand. "After a year at the U," she told him, "I'm going to transfer to Pasadena Playhouse."

Mr. Halloran just looked at her.

I Beat
the Midget

My old man got into the Shetland pony business by accident, when he traded a couple loads of pig feed to a fellow for a yearling Shetland mare. That was when I was six. In two years that mare had a colt, and the old man picked up a couple more ponies on trades, and from then on they multiplied worse than rabbits. By the time I was sixteen and a sophomore in high school, the old man must have had fifty ponies. He left them shift for themselves out in the southwest pasture—he had a little spread about fifteen miles north of Billings, Montana, in those days—and those ponies holed up in the sagebrush and cutbanks, summer and winter. They were wilder than antelopes. You'd be riding through that pasture, and crash! A little bunch of colts would leap up out of the sagebrush and tear off, wild-eyed. Most of them had hardly seen a human. They were tough and ragged, inbred and every crazy color mixture, splotched and pintoed, with manes full of burrs sticking out in every direction and hiding their eyes. They were little—three or three and a half feet at the withers, most of them—less than waist-high on a man, but tough! I've never run into any animal since that was tougher than those wild Shetland ponies of my old man's.

There got to be more and more of them, with the fillies growing up and having colts of their own, till I guess the old man started to wonder if the southwest pasture was going to hold them for long. There aren't a whole lot of things you can do with a wild Shetland pony. A no-good horse, you can always sell as a canner, but not Shetland ponies. They only weigh two-three hundred pounds.

So it struck the old man that a good thing to do with these ponies would be to catch some of the younger ones and gentle them, and sell them as kids' pets. You could get fifty to a hundred dollars for gentle ponies then. Of course, my old man was too busy with the pig feed and skim-milk calf business to bother with ponies himself, but he figured that gentling them down would be just the chore for me.

So I started gentling ponies. That was the summer I had wanted to try out for the American Legion baseball team in town—they had a good ball club in Billings, those summers, and I wasn't a bad catcher—but nothing would do but I had to spend the summer fighting those ponies.

Jesus! How I got to hate Shetland ponies. I was at that age where I was starting to see that the old man and his pig feed route didn't stack up for much, and the pony business didn't look much better. It took me the first two weeks of June to run enough of the little bastards out of the sagebrush so I could cut out some colts. I rode that pasture in ninety-degree heat with a Levi jacket and the old man's batwing chaps, but I still had thorn cuts and a lot of bruises from the scrub pines. Old Beauty, the chore horse, was sorefooted by the time I had those colts cut out, and I was ready to quit right then.

The old man's theory of horse-breaking, which I used on those ponies, was the old-time bronc-stomper approach, the old man having been a cowboy before he got busted up and got married. First you got your animal into the round corral, and you chased him around and around for most of an hour, if you were as poor a hand with a rope as I was, trying to front-foot him. That summer I finally got so I could snare a pony eventually, even when I couldn't actually lasso him. The old man would sit on the top corral pole and cluck about how he could rope when *he* was sixteen. But snaring worked out the same. When that lariat hit a wild pony's feet, he'd let out a squeal like a pig getting gelded, and then he'd go straight up in the air, come down and go up again. You'd of thought he was a goddamn rubber ball, the way he'd bounce.

This would go on for an hour or so, me jerking the pony's feet out from under him every time he got up, and him hitting the corral dust and bouncing and going straight up, till my arms were about ready to come out of their sockets, and his knees had the hell skinned out of them, and he stopped jumping and started sulking instead. Then I'd spook him over one more time, so he'd land on his side, and the old man would climb off the top corral rail and help me hog-tie him. Then I'd start the second step in the old man's horse-training program.

That was to get a gunny sack out of the chicken house and flap it all over the hog-tied colt, until he stopped wincing at it. Sacking out, the old man called it. He said that after a day or two most broncs got over shying at the sack. But those damned ponies never stopped. They'd get kind of numb and dazed after a while, but after an hour's rest they were as spooky as ever.

After I got a pony sacked out, I'd tie him to a corral post and leave him there overnight. The old man's theory was that the pony'd wear himself out fighting the post and see that he couldn't get away. Therefore, when I went to lead him to water the next morning, he wouldn't fight me any more than he'd fight the post.

But these ponies did one of two things. Either they planted their feet and let their eyes roll back in their heads and let their necks stretch, until I was practically dragging them along with all four feet rigid, or else they followed right along, watching for a chance, and wham! They'd hit the end of that rope, and it'd rip through my hands, taking the skin with it. The old man just shook his head. Never saw such stubborn little bastards, he said. I knew I hadn't. I just kept dragging them to water, wondering how the guys were coming out at the ball park, and cursing the old man.

Once they were halter-broken, or at least were at the point where I could drag them to the water trough and back without taking the rest of the skin off my hands, it was time to start riding them. That was the real circus. Oh, Jesus.

You can't get a saddle to stay on one of those ponies. At least, I never could. They haven't got any withers at all, and their skin is loose and rolls like a mutt dog's. After a couple of saddles had ended up under their bellies, I started riding them bareback and taking my chances.

There's nothing quite like riding a Shetland colt, I swear to God. You don't have hardly anything to sit on, and nothing to get a knee-grip on. You can feel that bundle of springs down there, bouncing around and throwing its head back and trying to split your balls, but all you can see is this mess of streaked black and brown and white mane, and once in a while an ear sticking up through the hair. Being so short-legged, of course they've got no gait, even when you've got them lined out in one direction. They just jar up and down. And buck! They can turn inside out in midair.

Somehow or other I got three of those colts about half-way broke to ride that summer, though I never could really lead them, and the old man took them down to Wyoming and peddled them for fifty bucks apiece. I wondered what kind of kids got them, and what they did with them. I didn't care much, though, because I was so glad to get rid of them. They were too damned ornery, and even after they got part tamed, I hated riding them. It wasn't just the jar-ring. My legs hung way down past their knees, and I knew I looked like some kind of fool. If any kid I knew had seen me, I'd have died. It would have been worse than having the old man hauling his pig feed around town. Those ponies made me look like a big over-grown lummox, even though there wasn't a one of them that didn't buck me off at least twice. I had more bruises that summer than I ever got playing baseball.

Well, my old man sold the ponies and counted his money, and it looked good to him. But then he hadn't been bucked off and ploughed up any corral dirt with his face, and he still had the skin on his hands, and he hadn't been half-ruptured. He sent me out for another batch of colts. It was the middle of August, and he figured I could get a good start on them before school started. So I went out and combed the sagebrush again on old Beauty, cursing the old man under my breath till I got out of earshot, and then cursing him out loud. I finally ran in another little bunch of ponies. And that was the time I really made a mistake, because one of the ponies in that bunch was the Midget.

The Midget was a full three-year-old, the old man said. That was later, when we'd tied him down to castrate him, and the old man could get a look in his mouth. He was still a stallion when I brought him into the corral that first time, and showier than any of the others. He was a bay and white pinto, with black streaks in his mane and tail, and he had a way of arching his neck and challenging you from across the corral like some wild desert stallion out of a painting. And he looked a little like an Arabian, with that arched neck and dish face. Except he was pinto, and coarser built, and pint-sized. He was in good shape (Shetland ponies can keep fat anywhere, even on sagebrush) and with the sun shining on his bay coat, he was a pretty sight to see.

So, because I liked his looks and the way he held his head, I kept him in. I should have known better. I should have kept in the scrawniest, raunchiest ponies in the bunch. They'd have at least given me an even chance.

I hazed the others out and left the Midget alone in the round corral. He didn't have a name then, just the bay and white stud. The old man started calling him the Midget later on, to badger me when I had such a fight with him. He stood across the corral with his head up, looking through his foretop at me, uneasy about the lariat I was coiling.

"Jesus," said the old man from the top rail. "He's got a chest on him. He'd make a rope horse if he was just full-sized. You better watch that little bastard, Jimmy."

I got my rope coiled and built me a loop. With the old man watching, I usually made two or three tries at front-footing a colt. The Midget had his tail against the fence, moving his feet like a boxer and watching that rope.

"Hah," I said, slapping my leg to get him running. "Hah, get outa there."

To front-foot a horse, you get him running along the corral fence, and you snake your loop right in front of him. Both front feet go in, and you set yourself and bust him over on his nose. But you have to get both front feet. Just one, and you don't have much control. And you have to jerk him off balance. It's all in the timing. The old man claimed that in his cowboying days, he could front-foot a horse just right and break his neck. I never saw anybody do that. Not on purpose, anyway.

"Yah," I yelled at the Midget, and he spun away from the fence and tore past me, kicking up dust and little chunks of dried manure. I swung my rope and missed by about ten feet. The old man sat up there chortling while I dragged my loop in and coiled it up again.

The Midget watched. He wasn't rolling-eyed and shivering like the other colts. Just ready, kind of easy on his feet, like a pro getting set to steal second base.

"Look at him," the old man growled. "Acts like he knows what a rope's all about. Wonder if them goddamn kids from town've been comin' out and runnin' them ponies."

I didn't know. I got my loop ready again, and I hazed the Midget away from the fence. He started to stampede past me, then swapped directions and came right at me, ears flat. I yelled and gave my loop a heave in his face. For a minute all I could see was hoofs and the shaggy hair on that pony's belly. Something whacked me in the ribs, and I yelled again, and then I could see blue sky and clouds right over me, but I didn't have time to look, because the rope was going through my hands and jerking me over in the dirt. The Midget was at the other end of that rope, making it whang. I'd caught one front foot just by accident as he charged over the top of me.

I got up and spat out a mouthful of dirt and straw and looked across the corral. The Midget stopped and looked back, waiting.

"Jesus Christ!" the old man howled. "If I'd ever let a little bitty snot knock me ass over teakettle in the middle of a corral, I'd of drawed my walkin' papers. Stumbled-footed kid! Baseball!"

"You want to try?" I asked him. He just cackled.

Somehow I either had to get that rope off the Midget's foot or else manage to bust him with just one, and either was going to be a hell of a fight. The old man just sat up there and grinned. Since my mom died, there'd been nobody to make him clean up once in a while, or change his clothes. I looked up at him, grinning down at me all bewhiskered and toothless, with his upper teeth weighting down the front shirt pocket where he carried them, and I wished I had him on the other end of a rope.

The Midget waited, ready to jump in either direction, while the sun burned down on his shiny bay coat and on the corrals and the trampled-down grass in the yard, and reflected off the broken window in the old man's truck. The sweat was running down the back of my neck and on down my spine, and I didn't want to mess with that pony. He wasn't even scared, not like the others. They might kick or bite or stampede, but that was because they were afraid. Not him. He waited. The minute I moved that rope, though, I could tell he was tense.

I figured my best bet was to try to bust him with his one foot in the rope. Maybe I could get him down without getting kicked myself. And if I didn't, maybe he'd kick off the rope, and I could start all over again.

I shook the rope. "Hey! Hah!"

The Midget just stood there, so I took a run at him and flapped my hat. He jumped sideways then, but instead of stampeding away and hitting the end of the rope hard, he dove around me in a circle.

"Watch out, you're gonna get tangled in that rope!" the old man whooped. I didn't have to be told that. Another few feet and that damn pony would have had a turn of the lariat around my middle. I ran with him, we were both running in a tight circle, and the old man was laughing. I finally made it to the corral fence. The Midget stopped and arched his neck at me.

"Hoo!" The old man was wiping tears out of his whiskers. "Hee! Baseball!"

My hair was hanging down in my eyes as bad as the Midget's, and sweat was getting in my mouth, and I was ready to kill the old man. Him or that pony, one or the other. There he sat, laughing at me under his greasy hat, just because I was no cowboy and wanted to play baseball. Damn it, I was a pretty fair catcher, it was what I wanted to do, and a hell of a better way to spend my time than fighting Shetland ponies and maybe going into the pig feed business. I lunged at the Midget again, whooping at him, and this time he did stampede, right at me. I ducked, tasting dust and fine manure again as he went over me, and more trying to get out of his way than to bust him, I leaned into the rope. I couldn't see for dust, but that rope stretched out and hummed and jerked me over on my back.

I rolled over to get out of the way of the rope, but it wasn't tight, just jerking like hell. The old man had scrambled down off the corral fence and landed on the Midget's head. The Midget was squealing and kicking, making that rope whip like a rattlesnake in a fit, but he couldn't get up. You sit on a horse's head, he can't get up, and you're safe as long as you lean back far enough that he can't reach up with a hind foot and kick you in the teeth. The old man was leaning back, grinning from ear to ear, with a good grip. The Midget could kick all he wanted.

"We'll cut this sonofabitch," the old man cackled. "That'll take the starch out of him."

We hog-tied him, finally. With all the old man's blowing and bragging, the Midget was all he wanted to handle. We were both dripping sweat and the Midget was wet all over by the time we had him fast. Then the old man got out his whetstone and jack-knife and started sharpening it while I built a little fire out of pitch-pine.

The vets would come out and geld a stud for you, but they charged twenty-thirty dollars and mileage, and of course the old man wasn't going to go for that. He took a chance of his horse bleeding to death or dying of lockjaw, but I've known of horses bleeding after the vets finished with them. And it wasn't like one of those Shetlands was worth much to start with. Anyway, the old man always seared the wound, and he had pretty good luck with the colts he cut.

With a calf, you can just castrate him and shake on some powder to keep off the flies, but with a horse, you've got to sear the big blood vessel shut to keep him from bleeding to death. So I built my little fire out of pitch-pine and heated a branding iron while the old man spat on his whetstone and sharpened his knife.

"Got a lot of jewels here for a little snot," he said, and went to work with his knife.

I didn't know how I felt about it. I knew the Midget would be easier to handle as a gelding, but still he'd been a pretty sight with the arch in his neck and his head up. And I'd read the horse books when I was a kid, all about this stallion or that, that some kid tamed. But they at least had had horses they could ride in public, some wild desert stallion or island stallion, not like this half-pint fire eater I'd drawn. So I stood there and watched until the old man had finished and thrown the testicles to the dog, that wasn't supposed to go near the corrals but hung around anyway, and then I fetched the old man the branding iron. The Midget hardly moved.

"Okay, Jimmy," said the old man finally. "Let him loose and turn him in the lower corral. He can get a little green feed there, and you can try him again in a day or two."

I opened the gate to the lower corral and then untied the Midget. It took a couple kicks to get him on his feet, but once he was moving I got him hazed into the lower corral without any trouble. He wandered down by the creek and stood there with his head hanging. I watched him off and on for the rest of the afternoon, while I worked with the other colts, but he didn't move. Once in a while he'd lash his tail at a fly. A little blood had trickled down the insides of his hind legs, and I wondered whether the old man had got him seared all right, but as the afternoon went on I could see it was drying and caking. By evening the Midget had left the creek and was hunting a little grass, so I figured he'd be all right.

He was more than all right. The next morning I went down to the corral before breakfast to see how he was. He was grazing, but his head shot up when I came around the barn, and I could tell he was poised, watching to see what I was going to do. You wouldn't have known anything had happened to him.

"Yep," the old man cackled, "he's waitin' for you all right."

I left him alone all that day, telling myself that I wanted to be sure his wound was healed. It wasn't till the afternoon of the next day that I opened the gates between the corrals again and hazed him through. There wasn't any drooping, one-foot-after-another. He went through the gate at a hard trot, eyes on me all the way. The colt I had tied outside nickered to him, and the Midget threw back his head and nickered back.

I closed the gate and started working the kinks out of my rope, taking my time. The Midget stood with his tail against the corral poles and his head up and facing me, waiting until I was ready. The instant I had that lariat gathered up, he went tense.

I built my loop and started towards him. I didn't want to catch him, I didn't want any part of him. The old man had gone off with a load of junk to peddle at an auction, but he might just as well have been perched on the top rail. I could almost hear him cackle. It was hot, nearly a hundred degrees, and the sweat was running down my arms and chest and collecting around my belt. The Midget was crusted with salt where his sweat had dried.

After I'd tried to front-foot him and had missed four times, though, the Midget was running fresh sweat and breathing hard. I was blowing, and I had a sideache, and I was positive that I was never going to front-foot that snaky little bastard, not if I practiced the rest of the summer. The first time, the time I'd got one front foot, had been by accident. And the Midget was cagier now than ever, ducking back and forth, doubling like an eel and keeping an eye on the loop. He was skipping past it and making it look easy. I was licked.

It occurred to me that if I couldn't front-foot him, maybe I could rope him around the neck. He wouldn't be expecting it, so the first time, at least, I'd have some advantage. What I'd do once I had him roped around the neck, I didn't know. But at least I'd have him *caught.* The old man wasn't going to be gone forever, and he was going to have plenty to say when he found out I couldn't even snare that pony.

The sun was raising blisters on the back of my neck and glaring off the side of the barn so I had to squint into it. The Midget just watched me as I coiled up my last loop. Damn him, if I could once get my hands on him, I'd kill him.

"Yee-hah!" I yelled feverishly, and swung the loop. The Midget looked wise and sidestepped, lifted his forefeet daintily over the spot where the loop was supposed to drop, and snaked past me. I let the coils slip through my fingers at the last possible second, saw the loop go up and settle over that shiny neck. Just as I'd half hoped and more than half feared, the Midget had expected me to try for his front feet again, and now I had him.

Oh, Jesus, did I. He hit the end of the rope and squealed, jerking his head back and taking another piece of skin off my hands, tearing back and forth with his neck muscles until my boot heels were jarred out of their hold. Then he flattened his ears, bared his teeth, and came right at me. I yelled, too, and ducked around the snubbing post in the middle of the corral. If I could get a couple turns of the rope around the post, I might choke the Midget to death, but he wouldn't run me down.

He knew what I was thinking, and he was right behind me as I dived around the post. Just once I thought his teeth were closing in on the small of my back, but only his nose grazed me, and I was around the post again. I stopped and leaned back on the rope. The Midget stopped too, braced, his breath rattling through the tight noose.

I didn't know what to do. I didn't want to see him choke to death right there before my eyes. Finally I took a couple half-hitches around the post and went and got a rope halter. Maybe I could get that on him.

He watched me coming back, his breath rattling huskier than ever. The side of his tongue was shoving out between his teeth, and foam was soaking into the dirt under his chin.

"Easy, boy," I said. My voice sounded pretty funny, but I didn't like to hear him breathe like that. I reached out, being careful to keep the post between us. He didn't move. I edged the halter a little closer to his nose, working it down, trying to get it under his chin. The Midget's eyes were glazing over, and I wondered if he was really choking to death. Then I had the halter under his chin and started easing it up. Another inch and the top of the halter would be flopping over his ears, and I could fasten it. I eased up, the halter flopped against him, and then the world turned red.

I didn't know where I was, except that everything was moving in a crazy direction, and the Midget's teeth were in my belly, and one foreleg seemed to have got wrapped around my ribs, and somewhere miles away that fool dog was yapping like a maniac. I still had the halter in my hands, it was still over the Midget's head, I was buckling it, and then something smashed into my nose and I thought I'd been split in half. Then I was flat in the corral dust, and the Midget was braced at the other end of his rope, rattling, the halter in place. Something warm was making my neck sticky and darkening the corral dirt under my face. I put up a hand to see if my nose was still there, and it came away full of blood.

It was the sight of my own blood that set me off, but there was more to my explosion than that. All of a sudden, sitting there in the corral with the sun clotting the blood on my face and my head ringing, everything came together: that damned pony, my catcher's mitt getting stiff in my dresser drawer, the old man and his dirty whiskers, and Pauline Ledbetter snickering at our pick-up driving past the school. I hated the old man, I hated the Midget and the whole tribe of worthless wild Shetlands, I guess I hated myself. There was an old singletree just outside the corral gate, two and a half feet of cured oak with six inches of chain attached to one end, and the next thing I knew, I had it and was laying the chain end of it across the Midget.

I beat him until my arm was numb. He jerked back on the rope until his eyes bugged out, but he couldn't get away, and I brought that singletree down on his head, nose, back, legs—once I caught my own legs with the chain on the rebound, and that made it all the worse. Somebody was cussing, screaming, crying, in a funny high voice, and it was me. I beat, and I beat, and I beat, and I liked it. I liked those welts to rise out of that smooth skin, I liked the blood to run, I liked to see him brace back on that rope while the blood and sweat mixed and his eyes filmed. I beat until my arm was numb and I couldn't feel the singletree in my hand any more.

Then I stopped, and I looked down at the singletree. It was like somebody else's hand was holding it. I didn't know who I was, but I was somewhere outside of Jimmy. Jimmy, that poor slob, was standing in the middle of a corral with blood running down his face and holding a bloody singletree. I was looking down at Jimmy and at the bay and white and bloodied pony and hearing a meadow lark whistle from a pile of junk on the other side of the corral. The sun was blazing down on Jimmy, but it wasn't touching me.

After awhile I dropped the singletree and fetched the powder we'd used to keep the flies off the Midget's balls. I shook it on the worst of the cuts, and he just stood there, not even shuddering when I touched him. Then I got my knife and cut the rope. The Midget took a step back and staggered. I opened the gate to the lower corral and hazed him through. He could get water and green feed there, and some shade. Then I went to the house and cleaned up my own face. I still wasn't feeling like myself.

The old man came home about dusk. He saw the Midget

grazing, and he looked at me, but he didn't say anything. He looked around the corrals, but he never did say anything.

In fact, he didn't say anything more about Shetland ponies. The Midget stayed in the lower corral while his cuts healed, and the next week the old man made a deal with a promoter to take the whole herd off his hands. The promoter was collecting stock for junior rodeos, and he wanted the ponies for bucking stock. I didn't even help drive the rest of the ponies out of the sagebrush. The old man and the promoter did that. Then they loaded them up and trucked them off. Midget and all. We never saw any of them again.

The old man and I got along better after that, even though I lived at home until I was old enough to enlist. But I've never had much to do with livestock since then. It scared hell out of me that day, seeing the kid I used to be standing there in the sun with a bloody singletree in his hands, while this stranger in me watched.

Album

Successive ice ages had shaped the land, as though a careless sweep of clawed fingers had gouged the still malleable plains into plateau and valley. Thus cruelly torn, the land became harsher. The hills lay bare under the sweep of the galaxy, waiting from the beginning of time until the end. These years, wheatfields rolled their seasonal gold across the prairie, a momentary phenomenon that soon would be gone. Already the fine dust of the hot season filtered over fields, fences, and the fragile tracks of men.

The river bottom offered some protection. Here, at the foot of a narrow road through the bluffs, willows grew along the water. The milk cow and her heifer had found shade at the foot of their pasture, where they waited, switching flies and watching the house for signs of milking time. Nearer the buildings the hens clucked their concerns of the moment from their dust nests under the chokecherries.

The white frame house and its little patch of lawn were overhung by a seventy-year-old maple. The tree was one of several saplings that had been brought hundreds of miles by buggy; only this one had survived the first killing winter, but now it spread patterned green shade over the porch where the women sat, and had sprouts of its own around the base. Like the women who sat in its shade and rocked, the tree had settled into a bitter world for the course of its span.

Two of the women on the porch were white-haired. They resembled each other, though in fact they were related only by marriage. Both were physically strong women; they both had light blue eyes—childlike eyes, the young woman thought—and wore starched homemade dresses. Years of chores in garden and barnyard had left their arms and faces as brown and seamed as walnuts.

The thinner of the two old women jumped to her feet with surprising ease and shaded her gaze with her hand.

"That cat's got kittens hidden somewhere. Look at her, there she goes to the barn with another mouse."

The other old woman, her sister-in-law, continued to rock. "I expect the place can hold another batch of kittens, Dorothy."

"They'll grow up wild and bother the hens."

"Jeff's little girls will tame them when they come to visit."

"They'll be too much for the little girls. They'll be wild and spry by the time the girls get here," Dorothy countered, but her arguments had the lack of conviction of a spinster in the presence of a woman who has been married.

"Jeff's little girls have grown. I hardly knew little Peggy when I saw her at the funeral." The rocking chair's gentle motion continued. "So many of Lavinia's friends there, and so many flowers."

"It was the first funeral I ever went to where they didn't have the obituary read," objected Dorothy. "That surprised me. I wonder whose idea that was."

The young woman, Jean, who sat on the porch steps, was familiar enough with her great-aunts' patterns of response that she could have predicted every word, though it had been three years since she last had listened to them. The limitations of their conversation, the sunbaked barnyard, and the dark little house with its oilcloth and spotty floors depressed her as much as the desultory talk of her grandmother's funeral, only a week past. The visit with the two old ladies was paid out of duty and the memory of past affection; but already she toyed with ways to escape ahead of time.

"Jean begins to look like Lavinia, doesn't she?" her Aunt Emily observed unexpectedly. Her rocking chair continued its unhurried rhythm.

Aunt Dorothy turned from her observation of the gray barncat's doings and gave Jean a sharp, considering look. "I never thought of it before, Emily."

Emily laid her knitting in her lap and rocked on. Her blue eyes were faraway. "I was thinking about Lavinia and how she looked at the time she taught at the Bally-Dome. She was about the age Jean is now."

Dorothy looked critically at her great-niece. "The way you girls wear your hair now, all skinned back, and those steel-rimmed glasses! You'd be right in style for my day, Jean."

Jean smiled politely and tucked a wisp of brown hair behind her ear, but inwardly she felt familiar resentment rising that anyone could think that she, Jean, was what these old women once had been. Her own supple brown hands lay loosely in the lap of her short cotton dress; her aunts' hands, always filled with knitting or sewing or food or tools, were gnarled, stiffened with too much heavy work and scarred by work that was too dangerous. Aunt Emily had a deep mark on her wrist that Jean knew was a rope burn, and both old women could display nicks and troughs on their fingers that had been left by knives, mowing-machine teeth, or barbed wire. Any prettiness that they might have had, they had used up right away, Jean thought with resentment. It was as though prettiness were something to be left behind as soon as possible; and she looked with protectiveness at her own smooth fingers.

Emily resumed her knitting. "I always thought Lavinia was the prettiest of Edward's sisters."

"Pretty is as pretty does," said Dorothy sharply, but she was ready to yield to the pleasure of reminiscence. "I was ten years old when you married Edward and came here to live. We all had new dresses for the wedding, and all the neighbors came—I remember the buggies coming across the ford. Alice was fourteen then, and Lavinia was eighteen."

And now there were only Emily and Dorothy, Jean supplied to herself. Alice dead in young womanhood, Edward in middle age. And Lavinia, her grandmother, buried last week. And yet the voices of the two old women were as undisturbed and light, dropping off into the sunlight as inconsequentially as the clicks of the knitting needles or the unruffled sounds of the hens in the heat of the day.

"Doesn't it bother you to talk about them?" she demanded without thinking, and bit her lip the next moment; but the old ladies exchanged indulgent looks over her head.

"Now, Jean, what will be, will be," said Emily gently, and Dorothy nodded her small white head from her seat on the porch railing. Jean again felt the resentment rise, but her aunts' voices pattered on.

"Hard to believe Lavinia was ever as skinny as Jean."

"She wasn't," Dorothy objected. "None of us ran to skin and bones the way the girls do today. We all had flesh."

Aunt Emily knitted on decisively. "Dorothy, you don't remember. Lavinia had an elegant slim figure as a young woman. It was after she was married and the babies came and things were so hard out there on the homestead that she went to flesh."

Dorothy looked mulish. Then she slid off her perch on the porch railing and crossed to the door with her surprisingly easy steps. "I'll just get Mama's album."

Aunt Emily knitted on, but her mouth twitched. It was the closest she ever came to a smile. "My mother-in-law—that was your great-grandmother, Jean—used to say that Dorothy could never sit still long enough to get married."

Dorothy came back through the screen door, carrying the large plush-covered album. She looked suspiciously at her sister-in-law. "Guess I can sit still. Doesn't mean I wanted to get married, though."

Jean knew the album from childhood. The dusty blue plush under her fingertips recalled sticky afternoons on Aunt Emily's porch with her cousins, eating fried chicken and giggling over the clothes and stiff postures of their elders, while the originals of many of the photographs drowsed in the parlor after their Sunday dinner. Some of the faces in the album she still could name, not because she could associate these youthful lines and planes with the people she had known (in almost every case the known face seemed to Jean to be so changed as to be completely unconnected with the early likeness), but from summer afternoons of clamoring, "Who's that, Aunt Emily? Who's that in the buggy? On the fence?" It was inconceivable, for example, that her own grandmother, whom Jean had known as a broad, silent old woman with painfully misshapen feet and joints, ever could have been the startled child whose high woolen collar seemed to be throttling her. Or that her grandfather, that mysterious suspendered mountain wheezing in his chair, had a counterpart in the narrow-chinned youth peering slyly at the camera from beneath his greased wings of hair.

To the child, there simply had been no connection between the fading likenesses and the known flesh; that Aunt Emily always replied to the constantly reiterated "Who's that?" with "That's your Aunt Dorothy when she started school in town," or "That's my father with his buggy horse, and the boy holding the halter went away to fight in Cuba and was killed," or "That's your grandfather when he first filed on the homestead," was only a game in which Aunt Emily always managed to parry the child's unbelieving questions with an outlandish but unassailable answer.

The young woman, however, began to see remembered likenesses as her aunts turned the crumbling black pages. Here a tilt of a head, there a scowl. Recognizing these faces of the dead somehow caught here for a little while in fading photographs pasted to album leaves that after seventy years were beginning to decompose, with names and histories remembered by the two old women (how long before the names went to the grave and the photographs became dust?) made her uneasy, and she looked off across the sunbaked barnyard with distaste.

Dorothy, who had forgotten her purpose in fetching the album, called Jean's attention to a posed studio portrait of four small children.

"Do you know which is your father?"

"The second one," Jean answered automatically. *Who's that, Aunt Emily?* But looking more carefully at the six-year-old boy in the constricting collar, she could see the line of eyebrows and nose, the set of the eyes, that would become the besieged outlook of the man.

Emily looked over from her rocker. "That picture was taken in March, just before they moved out to the homestead."

"The spring of the diptheria epidemic."

"And Jeff was born that summer."

After the little girls died of diptheria, Jean added to herself. The children stared out at the photographer, pale above their unnaturally confining clothing.

"How did she stand it?" she cried. "She had eight children and lost five. Two to diptheria, two to influenza, one drowned. Living out there on the homestead for days and days without seeing anybody, and there isn't even a tree in sight. Carrying all her water a quarter of a mile, and Grandfather never ever talked, to her or anybody else—"

The old ladies looked at each other again, and Emily knitted carefully to the end of her row. "Things come to us, and we meet them. Your grandmother did her duty, same as we all did." She seemed to recognize that her words were untranslatable to her great-niece, and laid down her needles. She sat for a moment, turning her stiffened hands palm upward, and Jean remembered that Emily also had lost a child in the diptheria epidemic.

"Things pass," said Emily at last.

Jean looked away. The sun beat on the little board walk, wilting the grass and Aunt Dorothy's row of sweet peas. Heat shimmered over the bare road and the dusty chokecherries beyond it. One chicken chased another with a ruffling of white feathers through the weeds on the other side of the fence, and the gray cat emerged from the barn, looking carefully in all directions before disappearing into the weeds on her own business. The dusty little circle seemed all at once not merely tedious, but suffocating. Of course, things passed. Their lives had passed with no more disturbance and less comfort than the lives of the chickens that Aunt Dorothy fed and that Aunt Emily would stew for Sunday dinner, one by one, or the existence of the cautious barncat, who would hunt for field mice until a hawk sighted her and plummeted successfully.

Jean took a deep breath. Her own life would pass, the days would dawn and fade, but at least she had had something. She plucked at the hem of her expensive cotton dress, noting again the flexibility of her tapering brown fingers, the glint of the sun on her handcrafted bracelet. Unlike her grandmother and her great-aunt, she had her job and her clothes, her records and books and her glimpses of what she still thought of as the "outside world," if not at first hand, at least through foreign films. She had lived in the city and visited coffee houses and discotheques, and she had slept with three men. All this Jean offered up as a shield between herself and the smothering energy of the sun. At least she had had experiences. Aunt Dorothy looked from her sister-in-law's face to her niece's and turned a leaf in the album. "That's Jesse MacGregor," she said. "He came over here from Scotland and herded sheep for my father. Your great-grandfather's sheepherder, Jean."

Jean had seen the picture before, but she looked obediently, squinting as sunlight fell over the page. The man leading a horse in the picture wore the drab clothing and heavy mustache that the child remembered. To the child, the unfamiliar face had been no-age, a face out of the undifferentiated limbo of grownupness. The young woman saw, as if through an overlay of memory, that Jesse MacGregor had an energetic cock of his head and high spirit in his face that turned, not toward the horse he led, but toward the photographer. Jesse MacGregor had been a young man on the day someone with a complicated camera had troubled to go through the ritual of recording the face of a hired sheepherder from Scotland.

"Lavinia took that picture," Emily said. "She bought the camera in the late fall, with the first of her school money from the Bally-Dome."

Dorothy looked sharply at her sister-in-law. "Jesse MacGregor was an awful man for the drink. Papa used to say that Jesse was a dependable man until he had the first wee drink. And then nothing could keep him until he'd finished his spree."

Emily pursed her lips. "Yes, he drank."

"Why, Emily! No one ever liked to speak in front of us girls, but I can remember as clear as yesterday, Jesse riding in after dark and singing out by the water tank, and Papa would get up from the supper table without saying anything, and go out—" Dorothy's voice dwindled. "Anyway, I don't think Lavinia ever *thought* about Jesse MacGregor—"

Emily started another row. "Jesse MacGregor was a dependable man, sober. I remember—"

Jean looked up to see that Emily had let her knitting fall into her lap again and was looking out at the bend of the river that could be seen through the willows.

"It was after I'd married Edward. Lavinia had to file on her homestead—the place on the benchland where your father lives, Jean. It was a thirty-mile ride to the county seat, too far for her to go alone, and the men were gone, Edward and his father—but Lavinia had to get in to the courthouse and she was getting ready for the ride, and her mother was nearly beside herself. And then Jesse rode in from the sheep camp that morning. It was time for his spree.

"So Jesse said he'd ride in to town with Lavinia, and then her mother *was* wild. But Lavinia said nonsense, she had to go to town, and if Jesse MacGregor rode one way with her, she might be able to find someone who'd ride back with her. Jesse caught a fresh horse and they started out.

"Mother worried all afternoon, and all evening, and all the next morning. But late on the second day, Lavinia and Jesse rode in. Jesse stopped at the corral, changed horses, and left again. Lavinia turned her horse out and came up to the house. We were all waiting in the kitchen."

Emily plucked at her ball of yarn with her thickened fingertips. "Lavinia said they'd ridden to town and that she had filed her claim. Then she went to her aunt's house for the night, wondering what would happen in the morning. But in the morning, Jesse MacGregor was at the door with her horse, cold sober. He rode all the way home with her, saw that she was safe, and turned around and rode thirty miles back to town for his spree."

"That's what drink can do to a man," said Dorothy.

"What happened to him?" asked Jean. She never had heard the story of Jesse MacGregor, or recalled anything attached to his picture but his name.

Her aunts did not answer. Dorothy turned her birdlike white head from side to side; Emily sat quietly withdrawn into her own thoughts.

"He was shot," Emily said at last, rousing herself. "He was shot while watching your great-grandfather's sheep, and no one ever knew who did it."

"Lavinia never gave him a thought," Dorothy insisted jealously.

"No," said Emily thoughtfully, "I don't think she ever did.

Certainly not from the day she met Jefferson Evers. But it was right after that—"

"No, Emily, you've got no business to think he did it deliberately, especially after all these years."

"Did what?" demanded Jean. "Who? My grandfather?"

"No, no," said Emily. "Jesse MacGregor. He went on a spree the day Lavinia got her engagement ring, and when he sobered up, he went up in the hills to the sheep. When they found his body, he was fifteen miles north, clear over on the Blackwell range."

"Now, Emily—"

"He knew that country well," Emily went on, as if Dorothy had not spoken. "And he knew how touchy things were getting about grazing rights. None of the men liked to discuss it in front of us, but it was rumored that the Blackwells had threatened to have any man shot who tried to steal grass."

Dorothy opened her mouth but Emily went on, her words falling as lightly, her voice as inconsequential, as when she had talked of Lavinia's funeral or the barncat's kittens. "Jesse knew what would happen from the minute he turned those sheep north, and all the days it would have taken to drive them into strange grazing land."

Jean looked down at the picture. Jesse MacGregor's face had faded after sixty years, but the outlines of his body still expressed vigorous life.

"He was quite good-looking, wasn't he?" she asked.

"He was considered a very handsome man," Aunt Dorothy answered, crimping her mouth. "But Lavinia never looked at another man after she met Jefferson Evers."

Rays of sunlight fell through the maple leaves and whitened the picture of Jesse MacGregor, but Jean could see the lines of the young man's shoulders, the angle of his hat, with her eyes shut. She wished suddenly that she could not.

"Did Grandma know—how he felt?" she asked, uncomfortable with a vocabulary she knew had far different connotations for her aunts.

Emily sighed. "I suppose she must have. We didn't talk of such things."

"She couldn't have married him," put in Dorothy.

"All he had were the clothes he wore. And his sprees—"

"He was always a man who liked being alive," said Emily.

It was late afternoon, and Jean could leave now, get away from the scent of mildew and dust and the infirmities of old women. Tomorrow she would take the plane back home, to her own apartment and her own concerns, her own life that she protected so carefully from the decay that had found her grandmother and her aunts.

The sun was still hot, but Jean shuddered with an unfamilar feeling of the cold. She would take back with her the story of her grandmother and Jesse MacGregor, and how Jesse MacGregor, a man who liked being alive, had deliberately turned his sheep north to unfriendly grazing land on the day her grandmother had become engaged to another man. Jean stood up and brushed off her skirt. The story of Jesse MacGregor seemed to her the first sign of the decay she feared.

"Lavinia never *thought* of Jesse MacGregor," Dorothy crooned. Jean looked up at the new note in her aunt's voice, but Dorothy was looking at Emily.

Emily rocked once, twice. The ball of yarn rolled out of her lap. "It was a long time ago," she said.

"Lavinia never thought—"

"No, no." Emily's knitting lay abandoned, a stitch or two pulled out from the unwinding ball of yarn. "Never Lavinia. I was the one who thought of Jesse MacGregor."

"Emily!" warned Dorothy.

But Jean ran the step or two down the path and picked up the escaping ball of yarn. The story of Jesse MacGregor had unwound farther already than she ever had wanted to hear.

Forby and the Mayan Maidens

It is your belief, I take it, that undertaking this narrative will, in shedding light upon my *alleged* role in Richard's death, allow me to sleep nights. I have no faith at all in the efficacy of this project. The events leading up to Richard's choice, insofar as they had to do with me at all, were a part of my adult and conscious life. I have no reason to feel guilty. It is the irrevocability of his turning from me that I simply cannot—allow myself to dwell upon.

But lest I be charged with unwillingness to cooperate in my own cure, I have begun this account, to use your words, of the authoritarian figures of my childhood. What a phrase! Its illogic is manifest, for all children stand in the shadows of giants. My particular giants, my parents, were ordinary farm people. I am the younger of two brothers. My brother, Miles, still farms the old ground. He and I remain on good, if remote terms. My father is dead, my mother senile.

It is not at all unusual for a man like me to come from such a background. Few of my graduate-school acquaintances, as I recall them, or of my present colleagues enjoyed the advantages of a cultured or even sympathetic background. My personal history is depressingly commonplace: the bookish and sensitive child, rebuffed and belittled by puzzled or contemptuous parents and playmates, turns more and more to the rewards of scholastic achievement that eventually leads to escape through a scholarship at the state university and thence to the teaching assistantship and the painfully acquired advanced degree which in its turn, if one is fortunate, returns one to the teaching position at the undistinguished four-year college. The infrequent rewards, the Richards whose sensitivity and promise provide one with the opportunity to perform the rescue that was once provided for oneself, must suffice. Hundreds, possibly thousands, can tell my story.

Reason enough for my reluctance to reexamine it. In my case I was fortunate to have a brother like Miles who, in fulfilling perfectly the expectations of our little community, lessened the need to press me into the same deadening mold.

As I think upon it now, however, I admit that few among those thousands can boast of overcoming an initial encounter with public education as stultifying as was mine. For even in my boyhood, rural schools were beginning to disappear from farming communities just as remote as ours. Hardly a one of those schools can exist today. In his Christmas letter Miles mentioned that our very school had recently been purchased by a neighbor and hauled away to serve as a grain bin. A far more useful function than it had served in many years!

It was their inability to hire a teacher, wrote Miles, that convinced the local school board to bow to the inevitable. High time, indeed. Even in my boyhood it was difficult to find a teacher who would accept a position isolated by miles of muddy or snowbound roads beyond even the reach of telephone lines, without plumbing and without electricity and with the very drinking water carried from the spring—do I bore you? Those teachers were hardly the authoritarian figures you imagined. Only the halt, the blind, the dregs of the profession would accept positions in the rural schools.

It was my brother Miles's teacher's dropping dead in his shoes before the astonished eyes of the school's ten or eleven pupils that delayed my own enrollment in school for two fatal years. I do not exaggerate. It was during those two years that I grew into myself—or are you curious about poor old Professor Wentworth who dropped dead? Do you want to know the details? I really know very little, having been only six years old and kept in the dark at the time it happened. I do know that Professor Wentworth was ninety years old when they hired him. He had had a respectable teaching career but at his age no town school would have taken a chance on him. He was spry and alert but he, too, bowed to the inevitable shortly before Thanksgiving. Miles had to be driven ten miles to a school in the next district for the rest of the year, and I, who should have started the first grade in the fall, was kept at home by my mother for two more years. She was worried, I suppose, about the effect the sudden death might have upon me. Its effect upon Miles? You may well ask. I've never known. Did he, I wonder, lie awake at night as I do and watch the electric streetlight outside my window bleach the unresisting elm leaves and slowly fade as they resume their daylight greens one more time?

Why, why in the name of God must I bother with all this? Can you tell me what point it has? Do you think I can possibly care about elm leaves or Miles or country schools? I was begotten, born, and will—should I be fortunate enough to follow Professor Wentworth's example—drop dead before the momentarily startled eyes of thirty freshman composition students. Meanwhile I cannot sleep. You have implied that you can grant oblivion in return for these details, and God knows it is an exchange I would make joyously if only I believed in its terms; what else could I ask at three in the morning when, brain aching from the unrelenting roller coaster of associations it can no longer contain, I prowl from window to window in the dark and note how still the leaves hang in the artificial light? If only I could ask him, talk with him, have ten minutes back out of all time to plead my cause—as I say, it is the irrevocability of a suicide that leaves the living without an alternative.

In any event, I was at last enrolled in school, the wife of a neighboring farmer having agreed to open ours. Large for my age, self-taught to read from my brother's schoolbooks, longing for school with a misplacement of expectations that is pathetic in retrospect, I was set up for disillusionment in a way no one recognized.

"I think he'll be all right," I remember my mother saying. I remember that she sounded doubtful, but memory is a notorious liar. Certainly it seems as though I recall perfectly her sharp voice and the line gouged between her eyes as she turned in the long September twilight to carry the supper dishes to the drain board—but do I? Of course it was September, it was time for school to start. Of course she frowned; her frown was permanent. But if, by one of the technological feats that have reduced our young to illiterate victims of a box of flickering shadows, I could witness a, so to speak, metaphysical videotape of my mother's kitchen on that September evening, what would I see? Or hear (assuming a sound track)? Was she doubtful? Angry? Relieved to get me off her hands?

I think I remember her turning as my father pushed back from the wooden table and lifted his cup of coffee in a hand horny and permanently grimed from his fields—"Why wouldn't he be all right? Only place for him. Goddamn kid would get himself killed if I let him around the machinery. Even if you could get his nose pried out of his book he'd forget his head if it wasn't for Miles keeping track of him. Miles, now—" Some of this diatribe he may have repeated to my mother on that September evening, some of it at other times. How I feared him, and feared the certainty of his voice and the wallop of his hand! His assessment of me was the assessment which my first schoolmates made immediately and which has been made of me repeatedly since then: in a world split between the real and the unreal, my only province lies in the latter.

Miles, for example, knew what to expect. He drove grain trucks up to the day school started. Then he submitted reluctantly to a bath and clean clothes— "If I could skip the first week, Dad, and help you finish harvest?"—but at last dug out his baseball bat and glove and cheered a little at the sight of them.

But I couldn't wait to get to school. I tried to get out of the car before it came to a full stop in the schoolyard that morning, earning me a shout from my mother, but my feet were on the sod by then and nothing could stop me. I stood in the dry September grass that was still knee high on the playground, squinting against the glare of the sun on white siding and smelling the fields of stubble and the dust that converged from the horizon from all directions upon one point.

The school was cool in the anteroom. Underfoot the old pine flooring was hollowed from the feet of hundreds of children. Under the row of coat hooks sat the earthenware water cooler with its tap at the bottom and its row of drinking cups on the shelf behind it. In the classroom itself, light flooded through a dozen long north windows and fell in blotches across the waxed floor and the rows of desks in graduating sizes that were connected with the back of each seat supporting the desk of the next. The blackboard was clean. At the front of the school was the teacher's desk and a large flag. At the rear was the oil heater. A door behind the heater led to the teacherage, as everybody but me knew. Perhaps even in that first excitement, something about the teacherage warned me off. I do remember its smell, yeasty and cramped from the generations of women who had lived and cooked for themselves behind the schoolroom.

"And this is Wayne," said my mother, catching me by the neck and pushing me forward with a smile so unlike her that I struggled to escape her fingers. "Oh yes?" smiled the teacher, and I got my first good look.

You understand, don't you, what a crime it was? From Miles's social studies and science readers I had not only taught myself to read but had also caught a glimpse, so I thought, of a heaven on earth made concrete in a third- or fourth-grade classroom presided over by a smiling Miss White or Miss Bell who guided twenty or so small companions all united in their desires to examine the sources of weather changes or common modes of transportation or the lives of children around the world. Do you understand what I imagined lay ahead?

Mrs. Skaarda had taught for several years previously at our school, its proximity to her home being, I suppose, its one attraction. She was considered to be a fine teacher with a proper regard for phonics, those tiresome objects whose unpredictable fallings in and out of pedagogical fashion so worry the parents of young children—Mrs. Skaarda, as I have said, was strong on phonics, and her willingness to teach at our little school was considered a stroke of fortune for the neighborhood until her unexpected illness forced her to a long stay in a distant hospital and brought about the hiring, after a frantic schoolboard meeting, of poor old Professor Wentworth. Miles, my senior by four years—and six grades ahead of me because of my late start—had already gone to school to Mrs. Skaarda and liked her. This fall, after nearly three years of an illness I never heard named, Mrs. Skaarda felt well enough to return to the school, and my mother thought it safe at last to enroll me.

I do not remember ever seeing Mrs. Skaarda before that morning. Unlike my mother and the other farm women, who were heavy-handed and heavy-hammed from work and fatigue and over-feeding, Mrs. Skaarda was a small slim woman with bones as insubstantial as a bird's. While considerably older than the Miss Whites and the Miss Bells of Miles's old readers, she radiated something of their storied warmth. Her hair was dark and her eyes, too, were dark and apprehensive in their setting of fine wrinkles. Her smile for me was tremulous: "And this is Miles's little brother? Wayne? Oh-h-h-h-h! We'll be fine!"

After all the parents drove away, Mrs. Skaarda rang a little bell and called the small children off the swings and Miles and the big Snapp girls and Charlie Connard away from the baseball diamond to crowd through the cloakroom into the fresh sun-dappled schoolroom to try out desks for size. Mine, I remember, had hardly room for my legs under it; as the year wore on I was continually being cursed by Shelley Snapp for tripping her on her way to the pencil sharpener, which I could not help, my desk having been assigned me because of my primary status and not my size. Yes, from that first day I was paired with Forby Weston.

But back to Mrs. Skaarda. As I recall her small, anxious face, the way she cupped her chin in her hands while her eyes searched our twelve faces for reassurance, I must ask myself again: how well do I really remember her? And I answer firmly: oh surely I remember her as she was! For on that first day, whether she knew it or not, I recognized a kindred spirit in her, a fellow sensitive in the land of the unfeeling. From the time when, instead of beginning an arithmetic lesson, Mrs. Skaarda leaned across her desk and began to tell us how glad she was to be well again and how she looked forward to learning with us, I knew her for what she was.

For Mrs. Skaarda, too, stood in the shadows of giants. Her professors at college, a man who taught her niece in a city school, the director of a theater group to which she had once belonged—her father-in-law, her sister-in-law—

"I begged her to understand the man was dying!" Mrs. Skaarda's tremulous whisper reduced us to silence as we sat in our rows between the north windows and the blackboard. "But it didn't matter to her! It didn't matter!"

The accounts of her conflicts, begun in lieu of opening exercises, swelled through the mornings and sometimes continued after we had eaten our sandwiches at noon. We were a willing audience, for none of us had heard such tales; and, as though by agreement, we never discussed what we heard with our parents or even among ourselves. More and more those long mornings and lengthening afternoons became a matter of awe among us. Mrs. Skaarda's brother was dying of cancer. Every morning she brought us reports, not only of the callousness of her sister-in-law, but of each step her brother took as he yielded his body to decay. "Cancer has its own terrible smell," she whispered. "I gag when I sit at my own brother's bedside. Anybody would. And to think that he must lie there, never able to walk away from the putrid smell of his own body! And we'll all come to the same thing in the end. Everybody in this room will someday be putrid!"

"I'd shoot myself before I died like that," said daring Shelley Snapp.

"It's all the same in the end," Mrs. Skaarda told her sadly.

A few days later she told us that her brother could eat nothing. For three days he had eaten nothing. Then it was a week.

"He can't eat nothing! He'd die!" said my brother Miles stoutly.

"They give him liquids through a tube," she explained.

"But it isn't enough nourishment to live on. He would starve to death if he weren't dying first of cancer." Then she told us the dreadful family secret: it didn't matter to her sister-in-law whether her brother died or not.

One morning she came to school red-eyed. "He's dead," she told us, and burst into tears. The youngest Snapp girl cried, too, and the rest of us tried not to cry. Only Forby Weston showed no emotion, and, not for the first time, I focused my anger on Forby, my companion in the first grade, for his lack of sensitivity. He sat coloring in his workbook and paid no attention. I had always disliked him for his appearance and his inability to read; now I whetted my dislike by staring at him. He was as large-framed as I, with pale skin and fishy eyes and a large mouth like a fish.

"I sat up with him all night," Mrs. Skaarda recovered enough to tell us as we waited, rapt, for more. "I held his hand. No one else would stay with him. It happened about three o'clock this morning."

The schoolroom was so quiet that I could hear the soft rub of Forby's crayon across the paper.

"Did you know that dead bodies fart?" Mrs. Skaarda confided. "His did."

After her brother died, Mrs. Skaarda became fearful. For a few days fitfully spent on ordinary lessons, her eyes searched the schoolroom, lingering on the three shelves of old library books I had already read from cover to cover, the wainscoted cabinet that held chalk and paper, the twelve of us in our three rows, and coming to rest more and more often on our old oil heater.

"If it exploded, it would kill us, of course," her voice broke the silence. We looked up hopefully from our science readers, blinking against the sunlight now strained thin through frost-covered windows. "They might be able to identify my body. My desk is on the far side of the room. But most of you would be mutilated beyond recognition."

We all turned to look at the glowing heater, once our ally against the freezing December weather that kept us cooped in the schoolhouse during recess, but now transformed into a squat smug force capable of blotting us all out of existence.

"If it started to explode, I'd jump up and run," said Shelley loudly.

"You wouldn't have time to run," said Mrs. Skaarda.

For the rest of the week before school mercifully was dismissed for Christmas, we all watched the oil heater and breathed as tentatively as we could. For as Richard once took pains to point out to me, it is the threat from the familiar, from the recognized companion, that is the true rack of anxiety. Not, of course, that those were his words—no. You do not need to hear his words. I will never rid myself of them, and that they are drawn from the impoverished vocabulary of his generation does not make them the less poignant. Let it suffice that not only did he hold me responsible for his growing estrangement with his background, but he found insubstantial what I could offer in return. But this you have heard before. I have, as I have said, no reason to feel guilty.

I must say! (For you see, I am determined not to stray long from the assigned subject.) Although I earlier described my first

52

educational experience as stultifying in the extreme, it strikes me now that in some respects, at least, Mrs. Skaarda's brand of education far exceeded the trite doses fed most farm children stuck in a snowbound country school. If I remember anything exactly as it was, it is the way we sat through those winter mornings, hands folded on our desks and mouths slightly ajar as we listened to the unfolding installment of the slow death of one of Mrs. Skaarda's relatives or of the details of Mayan sacrifice. And oh, yes! Her teaching went much further.

I had long thought of myself as one of Mrs. Skaarda's own, a member of a small loyal flock that stood firm against the insensitivies of the world. Gradually I became aware that all of us, however, were not of the flock. Mrs. Skaarda's eyes lingered more and more—no, not upon me, but upon Forby Weston.

Because of our common grade assignment, Forby and I were often enforced companions. We took the pail for water together when it was our turn. We were supposed, ridiculously, to be doing lessons together. And oftener than not we were paired in the recess games like Last Couple Out or Prisoner's Base that the older children taught us. Forby, although large for his age, was in fact rather better coordinated than I; my clumsiness had rapidly won for me the dishonor of always being the last chosen for sides (out of doors, mind you! In schoolroom games I was always first in spite of my age). "You may be the smartest one in school, but you're the dumbest one outside it!" Shelley Snapp once taunted me. Such designations come early, as you see.

Forby was content to sit quietly at his desk and color while Mrs. Skaarda talked to the rest of us, and for a long time he gave no indication of being aware of her increased scrutiny. Perhaps he, too, assumed that as one of the chosen he was safe.

"There is something the matter with Forby," Mrs. Skaarda confided to Shelley over the water cooler. I, eavesdropping as usual, turned with Shelley to look at Forby where he sat coloring peaceably in his spelling workbook. "Why does he always color with the black crayon?" whispered Mrs. Skaarda. "Or the brown?"

"Why don't you use the red crayon?" she asked Forby. I winced, for her voice held the forced good will my mother turned on her neighbors. "Okay," said Forby, picking up another crayon at random and going on with what he was doing. Mrs. Skaarda turned and shrugged significantly at Shelley.

Even in retrospect I can offer little insight into the mystery of Forby. I once tried to explain the incident to Richard—"He probably just didn't know his colors," said Richard. I was disappointed. I had looked forward to sharing the story with him; Richard, I had felt sure, would understand, if not the causal relationship that sent Forby crashing out of his small world, at least the effect his crash has had upon me ever since. But it was not to be. I misjudged Richard, as I have misjudged so many others. But to return.

At the time I only knew that Forby had unaccountably taken the place of the Mayan civilization in Mrs. Skaarda's interests. We had considered the Mayans with her for—days? weeks? I don't remember. Sometimes it seems as though we were occupied with the Mayans for most of the winter, and yet surely at one time or another we did ordinary lessons? Wouldn't my mother, or some other mother have become suspicious sooner than she did and visited the school? And yet I recall only the Mayans.

Mrs. Skaarda had lent to Miles, her favorite, a book about the Mayan civilization to read over Christmas vacation. He shared generous portions of it with me. One episode haunted me for nights. It had to do with the sacrifice of Mayan maidens into a pool thought to be bottomless until recently fathomed by curious archaeologists who fetched up skeleton after delicate skeleton of hapless children cast down to appease their ancestor the sun. I daresay neither I nor the now-forgotten author of the book understood the mythology, but no matter. It was important, he said, that the maiden be cast into the pool at the precise moment dawn cracked over the horizon. He himself was so fascinated with the maidens that one night he waited by the pool until sunrise and, with its first rays, cast himself into the pool (but survived the fall and swam out.) He said the pool smelled bad.

Mrs. Skaarda was, as I said, fascinated with the Mayans and their sacrifices until Forby claimed her attention. Loyally we shifted our attention with hers.

"There is something the matter with Forby," Mrs. Skaarda whispered to Miles. "I'm so thankful you're here." Such was her intensity that even my unimaginative brother looked at Forby, while I trembled in my impotent rage that it was to Miles her clouded eyes turned for reassurance. Who was Forby to cause us such distress? Fish-eyed Forby!

"If he were ever to—you know—lose control, it would be more than any one of us could do to subdue him. The insane have strength beyond all normal measures," she explained to Miles in her troubled whisper. "That's what I'm afraid of. That he'll slip over the divide and overpower us all."

By this time every pair of eyes in school was glued on Forby. Could we possibly have believed the child was insane? was Richard's question. I don't know. Perhaps more accurate to say that, stimulated by the vicarious threat of death and destruction and awakened to the promise of sacrifice, we suspended our disbelief for the course of the action. For who could say what Forby might do? Was it impossible that his was the pale mien of homicidal mania? And Forby gradually looked up from his crayons and his paste and his other simple pursuits to find a wall around him.

Within doors and out—for by this time winter had yielded to early spring mud—we all watched Forby. No longer chosen on anyone's side in games, he took to hovering at a distance of a few yards and pawing with his overshoes at the greening sod, while I, once the clumsy outcast, shone in a new role. For I, who had been Forby's peer against my will, was now privileged to be his licensed tormentor.

"Get away!" Shelley might bellow across the few yards of unthawing prairie grass at dumb, uncomprehending Forby in his thick winter coat and cap. "Keep away from us! We don't want you hanging around us, so quit being so stupid!"

But Shelley could do no more than shout; anything further would be "picking on the little kids" and outside the pale of country-school convention. But—"You chase him off, Wayne!" Shelley could urge. "Kick him. That's right. See? He's even scared of Wayne." And I, riding on a crescendo of encouraging yelps from the other children, ran at Forby and made him withdraw another ten or fifteen feet. "That's right!" "Kick him, he's got it coming!" they shrilled, and I raised an overshoed foot and planted its mud on Forby's undefended leg. For the first time in my life, I was flooded with joy. How thankful I was for Forby! How I fed my dislike upon his thick pale features! How I doted on his otherness that made me complete! Oh, the pure joy of my new mindlessness! How I capered in the April sun, freed by Forby from my old self as surely as though, snakelike, I had shed a skin!

As for what follows—the particular occasion when two mothers converged—that incident, as you will understand, I never confessed nor wished to confess to Richard. For it is one thing, is it not, to confess to the pleasure I took in another child's torment, but quite another to admit to its reverse? Why, indeed, continue now? Only because it is almost dawn and a few more paragraphs will suffice.

I even had some small part in bringing to an end my time in the sun, for I took to bragging of my exploits to my parents—little enough I had had to brag of in the past—at about the same time Forby's mother somehow divined through her son's phlegmatic exterior that all was not well with him, bringing the two women separately and coincidentally to school the day Forby was at last driven out of his skin.

Driven out of the circle and pelted with mud balls by the older children and teased and kicked and even bitten by me, Forby had made no attempt to defend himself. His eyes withdrew into the stolid white plane of his face as though no taunt, no pummel, could penetrate. But that day, I bolted my sandwiches and raced out of doors, quite beside myself in the mellow young sunlight—"Get away!" I shrilled at Forby. "Get away!" Screwing my face into ferocious indignation, I hurtled myself at the unmoving figure in the plaid cap and coat and decently buckled overshoes just like mine, only to stop in astonishment when he broke and ran.

After my first surprise, I ran after him, of course. We all ran, ten of us pelting across the mushy wet grass back of the school (Miles, whose presence might have made a difference, had taken to staying in the schoolhouse and talking to Mrs. Skaarda during recess), down the coulee that sliced the schoolyard and panting up the other side, gulping the sharp spring air that stung our young lungs, ecstatic because we saw we were going to corner Forby against the barbed-wire fence that separated the schoolyard from the neighboring grain fields—but the others had unaccountably fallen back and I was alone at Forby's heels when, instead of turning to accept his punishment from my hands, he crashed into the barbed wire and set it vibrating for yards in both directions.

Forby hung on the wires. Gradually they ceased their humming. Shelley and the others stood in a silent group. They had seen, as I had not, Forby's mother coming across the back lot. As I turned, she broke into a run with her coat flapping around her legs. She ran past me without looking at me and plucked Forby off the fence. Carrying him, she turned back toward the school. In his mother's arms Forby looked astonishingly long and limp.

The others turned and trailed in her wake back toward the school. I tried to catch up. "Did you see how dumb old Forby ran?" I tried.

Nobody would look at me. "You're the dumb one," Shelley muttered.

My mother and Mrs. Skaarda were waiting on the steps as we came around the corner. Forby's mother had put him in her car and had just slammed the door on him, but I caught a glimpse of his white face lolling against the seat.

I hardly dared to breathe, for Mrs. Skaarda's chin was trembling and her eyes were wells of fear. Even in that moment so indelibly etched that I can still remember the warm rotten smell of the spring thaw and the whistle of a meadowlark from the gatepost and the force of all eyes fixed on me, it was her fear I pitied.

Her hands were clenched in two small white fists at her waist. "I have been so worried," she said to my mother. Her voice shook. "I didn't know what to do. He's been worse and worse since the weather turned warm—hasn't he?" Her appeal was to my schoolmates. Solemnly they all nodded.

My mother's face was bright red. "You go in the teacherage," she said to me, "and stay there until we're ready for you."

I remember I took two steps toward the cloakroom door and stopped, still too dazed to cry or protest, to squint against the glare of eyes that pinned me there against the peeling white siding of the school. The realization, if not the comprehension, was dawning on me that it was I who was to be offered up to whatever gods she feared.

As I walked through the cloakroom and past the cold and harmless oil heater, I heard the burst of voices eager to tell what I had done. I walked into the teacherage and shut the door on all but an unintelligible buzz.

No one had lived in the teacherage since the days of old Professor Wentworth. The shades were pulled over the windows and a single beam of sunlight glared through a torn place. On the bed was a mattress. Mrs. Skaarda's coat hung on the back of the door.

I sat down on the bed to wait, where, in a sense, I have been waiting ever since. After a while, I got up and stood by the door and put my face against her coat. The moment on the steps, when I knew it was I who had been fixed outside the circle, had been as painful as a rotten tooth under a probe, but it has been the aftermath that has returned in the wake of Richard's choice to overwhelm me with its dim associations of dust and yeast. As you see, I can go no further. No, I am not responsible for Richard's death. It is the awful suspicion that once again the tables have been turned that keeps me here, blear-eyed but unable to sleep, as a raucous sunrise breaks into my window.

Granddaughters

"My mother marked all her granddaughters," my uncle used to say, and he said it again on the lawn that day, waiting for my cousin to come downstairs and be married. Caroline had chosen the garden at the ranch, at midsummer, for her wedding. That in itself was peculiar of her; other girls rented one of the churches in town and had someone sing "O Promise Me."

Now she was keeping everyone waiting. The great cottonwoods around the house threw patterns of sun and shadow across the grass that ran all the way down to the river. The wedding guests were dusty, and, except for my uncle, their voices were low as they waited, as always, for Caroline's own good time. The river bluffs that enclosed the ranch already had reddened in the afternoon sun, and still Caroline had not come down.

My uncle fumed, head lowered like a buffalo, his little eyes glaring out from under his thatch. "All like Ma, all four girls. She stamped every one of them, too damned independent."

"Oh, I don't know," said my mother nervously, because three of the four girls were her daughters.

My uncle watched the house with impatience. The curtains hung closed and limp at the second floor windows, and the double doors remained shut.

"Why the hell does she always have to do things the hard way?" he demanded after a minute. His sunburned hands were jammed into the pockets of his tuxedo, frustrated of the desire to grip his daughter and march her in the appointed direction.

"Well, now, Martin, at least she's getting married," said my mother.

"In her own good time," he growled. "She couldn't even do that like everybody else." Then they both turned and saw me, the real renegade, and fell silent.

I stood for a few minutes in the shade of the overgrown lilac hedge after they had walked on. From here I could listen to the river current, just quieter than the murmur of voices. My mother and uncle stopped on the dappled lawn a few yards away, still watching the house for signs of Caroline's coming down to undergo the ritual both of them depended upon to "make her see sense." My youngest sister was somewhere about, I knew, and my grandmother was holding court on the far side of the lawn.

From that short distance, my mother and uncle looked very much alike. Their coloring was different, but they held their stocky bodies in the same peering, anxious way. As I watched, they turned together to look across the lawn, and I saw that they had been talking about my grandmother, enthroned now in a lawn chair and brooding out over the gathering of her neighbors and descendents.

My mother and uncle professed to disagree with each other about nearly everything, and they quarreled every time they met. They both, however, lived in bitter awe of my grandmother; their youth apparently had been a continuous struggle to elude the old lady and her notions; their adulthood continued the rebellion by embracing the ordinary.

It was from their arguments, endlessly rehearsed, that I had learned most of what I knew about my grandmother. The old lady herself might tell stories, but suitably edited ones; in these accounts she herself emerged as a gracious lavendar-clad onlooker of the past ninety years, with no hint of the iron-jawed old despot who colored my mother's and uncle's rehashings. From their quarrels, I had pieced together a kind of sub-biography of a woman completely different from the old lady who had been so very kind to me.

The woman that my mother and uncle had fought had tried to avoid the salvation of what Everybody Else did, the comfort of doing what was expected of them, the reassurance of the enduring forms that, to their relief, Caroline was undertaking. This woman had, in 1896, forced her suspicious and disapproving father to allow her to put herself through high school and a year of teacher training by scrubbing floors. After a number of years of ruling school children in Sioux City, she had decided to marry a handsome young man who, before he quite had recovered from the shock of having a bride, found himself plucked from his comfortable Iowa dry goods store and set down among the alien hills of Montana to become, as best he could, a homesteader.

Of the four granddaughters, only I remembered that ineffectual consort, and my memories were vague, although I was ten years old when he died. My mother and uncle had despised him, though they took turns defending him in their quarrels with each other. My father spoke of him with affection.

Caroline still had not come downstairs. I had been standing alone too long; people were looking at me curiously from the other side of the lawn. Carefully keeping the heels of my shoes from catching in the grass, I began circling toward the group near the house.

My youngest sister intercepted me. She wore a pink linen dress that hung unnaturally over a frame that usually accommodated shirt and levis. The family had run so to girls that Lou had become my father's boy.

"What's it like being single again, Juley?"

Her eyes flickered over me, watching to see if she had hit a tender spot.

"Hello, Lou," I said.

She paused, considering me. Lou had had few enough advantages, growing up the youngest in the family by ten years. Now she was three inches taller than I, broad-shouldered, with square sunburned hands. In her battle against femininity, she had followed a pattern; I knew a dozen ranch women who lived in boots and blue jeans and spent their days in field and corral.

"How are the horses?" I asked Lou.

"One of the mares has distemper," she said glumly. "We spent the morning vaccinating the rest. Can't you smell it?"

Lou wore a minute diamond on the left ring finger. She had been engaged for two years to a young man named Tommy Blair, who owned a small racing string and an impoverished little ranch near my father's. Even before becoming engaged to Tommy, Lou, who was a natural horsewoman and a tireless trainer, had wrested control of the horses from him and set him to doing chores and keeping my father company.

"I told Caroline it'd be too hot out here," she said now, but her eyes still were on me. Lou told everyone what she thought, kept my father and Tommy busy, fought with my mother, even routed my father whenever he was unwary enough to give her an opening. Her record of unsuccessful skirmishes with me would not be enough to make her hold her tongue long. Already she watched me, wondering how much she dared tell me about my getting divorced.

"Have you heard from Karen recently?" I asked, to distract her.

Lou shook her head, her face changing. "Mother got a letter from her last month."

I looked away toward the river, and we both stood silent. Lou and I were too much alike, as openly stubborn as my uncle said we were, to be able to tolerate each other, and our affection for Karen was the one thing that tempered our antagonism. Karen's stubborn streak was different, but it existed.

Karen had been the good child, the pretty middle sister. My mother had loudly proclaimed the relief it was to raise Karen after my obstinacy, my living with my grandmother for months, my capitalizing on the old lady's money and encouragement to go to the university and from there to a marriage and a career that nobody understood. To my mother, I was a living contradiction to her own ordinary ranch wifehood, an ordinariness she thought Karen shared, that Lou claimed she shared.

Karen lived at home and helped on the ranch and worked as a part-time typist in the hospital in town. She was engaged, and my mother was pleased. But a year ago Karen had quarreled with her fiance, refused to discuss the details with anyone, and had gone away to Minneapolis. Minneapolis! Karen with a job in Minneapolis! It might as well be Moscow. That, and the broken engagement, had been my mother's largest concerns until I had numbed her by getting the first divorce in our family.

"Grandmother looks well," Lou said at last. We turned together and watched her in her chair across the lawn, hands folded across the knob of her cane. She wore lavendar silk and lace, and her hair was white, abundant and high-piled. Under this mass the high-arched dark brows still guarded her watchful brooding eyes.

"Mother says you wouldn't even have come home for Caroline's wedding if Grandmother hadn't written," said Lou with her little smile. It was the old pattern, her barbs making no marks on my skin that she could see, and her annoyance driving her to clumsier attempts.

"She's past ninety, after all."

"She looks like everybody's old grandmother with sugar cookies and a rose garden," Lou remarked. "Hard to think she was the liberated woman of her day."

I looked at Lou, as much surprised by the perception as by her giving up her attempts to anger me. Lou, who refused to consider alternatives to the foreman's job she had pre-empted from Tommy, how did she see herself?

"Are you a liberated woman?" I asked her, but that was going too far.

"That's all a lot of rot," Lou growled. "Some people don't know what marriage is all about."

So we were back to the barbs and the prescriptions, the shelter of the system from which Lou could ward off all threats.

Across the lawn, between us and the brooding old lady in the lawn chair, strolled and chatted the second cousins, connections by marriage, and long-time neighbors from up and down the river valley. Homesteaders, and their children and grandchildren, conservative enough that I actually could be, at thirty-five, the first divorcee they had nurtured. (Really the first? Surely I remembered a peripheral outrage or two.) These women in their best summer dresses were sunburned and creased, drivers of cattle trucks, midwives of lambs, assistant greasemonkeys. Their faces showed what they thought of me, who had run away to the university and depraved living; and also what they thought of Caroline, who also had run off to the university and dragged home a fiance, and now must keep them all waiting at her formal garden wedding while my uncle sulked in the first tuxedo he ever had seen.

My grandmother, of course, capitalized on her lace and lavendar, as though after ninety years of battling, she finally had invented a charming persona that permitted her to have her own way among her kin. It was not at all a bad feat for a woman past ninety; perhaps a strange one for one of the first women in Montana to cast a ballot. The forms, the forms that my mother and uncle and sister believed in, that Karen had fled from, had she bent them to suit herself?

"Hey!" said Lou suddenly. "Here she comes!"

I thought at first she was talking about my grandmother, who had not stirred, but it was Caroline who was finally making her appearance.

Not Caroline exactly, but the first of Caroline's bridesmaids was coming around the end of the house from the side porch, head tilted as though she could see no one, bouquet of roses and babies' breath held out aggressively in front of her. I did not recognize the girl.

"They're all Caroline's sorority sisters," hissed Lou.

I looked at her. "Did you want to be a bridesmaid?" Instantly I was ashamed of myself.

"That's a lot of rot," Lou retorted, and moved a few feet away from me.

The guests on the lawn belatedly had realized that the wedding actually had begun and were moving with the bridesmaids, slowly if they were near the procession and quickly if they had been loitering on the farthest stretches of the lawn. Briefly the lawn looked as if a flock of brightly-feathered chickens were hurrying to converge upon the girl and her basket of roses. I followed in their pattern, taking a step or two and waiting, moving again. The murmur of voices rose and fell, a whole complex accompaniment to the ceremony upon which everyone was converging.

Caroline had six bridesmaids, all dressed in tiered ruffles in shades of rose. I knew only one of the girls, a dimpled little redhead who had gone to high school with Caroline and on to the university with her. The fuchsia shade she had been allotted must have been a trial to her.

"Look at poor old Susan," jeered Lou, who had kept up with me. "Caroline can really be a bitch."

At this point Caroline herself appeared, drawing a fine gasp from the flock of wedding guests. The initial gasp was followed by a secondary reaction when everyone saw that Caroline had dispensed with being given away and had abandoned my uncle under the lilacs to squirm in his tuxedo.

The prime horror, however, was Caroline herself. Her wedding dress was a conventional pattern of tiered silk with a billowing traditional veil. Both dress and veil were a shade deeper than poor Susan's fuchsia. Caroline looked stunning.

Lou's mouth opened involuntarily, and I began to understand my uncle's earlier apprehension. One side of my mind recalled bizarre weddings I had read about, or been told about, similar accounts of which must have come to most of the people present; while another side registered the dumb amazement on the faces around me. Elsewhere girls might tease the tradition they obeyed by being married at the beach, on street corners, under viaducts, in see-through dresses, feathers, beads, fringe, but here? At the ranch? In red? Or was it really more of a purple? Caroline? As they recovered from their shock, every woman present was racketing up mental notes for her friends; the men simply were outraged.

"That bitch Caroline," Lou hissed at me, getting her wits back. "She thought old Larry was noticing Susan, so that's what she did to the poor slob."

"She did study to be a dress designer, didn't she? Maybe she's just showing everybody what she learned," I soothed.

Lou looked at me suspiciously, but whatever Caroline's plans, it was apparent from the set of her shoulders and the line of her mouth that she was having the day of her life. She was showing them all!

The minister, coughing and looking sidelong at the wedding guests, emerged from beneath the clematis at the back of the patio. Caroline's Larry waited on the flagstones, having got himself in the right spot at the right time without anyone's noticing him. It looked as if that would be his future calling. He was a frail, blond boy, almost as overpowered by his bride's sweeping silks as was the unhappy Susan.

Poor Larry, I thought. I could see that Lou was thinking the same thing. So were most of the wedding guests. But, looking at their faces under the green and golden light of the late sun, I was baffled. Here, in this quiet river valley where most of the pangs of the rest of the world were felt only at second hand, where the vows of this ceremony before us were taken for granted as stated, were men and women burned and seasoned with the labor of constructing their world. The very lawn I stood on was homesteader land, coaxed into greenness by water from the irrigation ditch that meant the difference between survival and death by dust and drouth. Every foot of this land had been tramped, fenced, and toiled over until it could contain this gabled house, this lawn where Caroline could spread her flaming silk.

And look what they had constructed! The minister had opened his book and was reading aloud, but I watched the people I had known since childhood. Hardly a man here who was not of homesteader stock, his values clear-cut, his hands toughened and begrimed with the battle with the earth. Surely, if ever men were salt of the earth, true inheritors of everything we had been given or taught, these were the men.

And hardly a woman here, hardly a woman who had not dug and sweated in the irrigation ditches, the hayfields, the machine sheds. It was not just the four of us who had inherited from my grandmother not the salt of the earth but an extra dose of stubbornness, a determination to hold out against the claims of a dearly-built world. Karen running away, Lou aggressively traditional, Caroline in her shocking silks, I with my divorce were a part of this world, kin to these women who now pitied and despised poor frail Larry, Larry who was about to take flaming Caroline in his arms for the bridal kiss. Watch out, poor moth, be careful of the flame. Caroline will find that it takes more than a red wedding dress to combat the strictures, and she will turn on you as a part of them.

My husband's voice, an echo of those three a.m. sessions of attack and rebuttal, floated above the formal questions and responses from the patio: *What the hell do you want from me, Juley? What the hell do you want?*

I don't want anything from you. I don't know what I want, I cried back.

"Do you, Caroline, take this man to be your lawfully wedded husband, to love, cherish, and obey—"

—You're too strong, Juley, you're too tough. You'll never break. And you'll never give in to me—
—I can't, I cried.
—If I'm afraid, if I'm unsure of myself, it's because you taught me to be.
—I didn't mean to, I cried.
"—and be true to each other, for as long as you both shall live?"

Karen in flight, Caroline in her flames. Lou in her corral exercising a yearling colt with a lead and a whip, my mother, my second cousin, how many other women in the bitter cycle of planting and harvest, complaining and compromising, resolving to make do. What can't be cured must be endured. I with the recriminations in the night, an affair, a divorce, an end of the affair. What was the matter with us, that we must beat or tear or shock or rage to find our way out of our inheritance, only to find ourselves in another fold?

The ceremony had ended. The minister retreated to the clematis; a receiving line began. Larry's cheeks caught the last sunlight in a furious blush.

"Look at him," sneered Lou.

A distant cousin had not noticed Lou and me standing behind her. "Look at the poor sucker," she said to her neighbor. "What do you bet Caroline drives him crazy? Her grandfather died in an asylum, you know. They say the old lady drove him to it. She's a tough old hussy."

The neighbor saw us and coughed. "How's the crop going to be?"

"Oh—fair, I guess. He never got around to drilling when he should have, you know how he is—"

"Yes," said the neighbor heavily. They moved on.

Lou joined the receiving line, moving purposefully toward the radiant Caroline. I followed her for a few steps, then slipped out of line and crossed the grass to the old woman in the lawn chair.

"Hello, Grandmother."

The hooded eyes lifted; the deep downward lines lightened in a smile.

"Well, Juley."

"How have you been?" The questions I wanted to ask her were jumbled together in my head.

Her smile lingered. "Very well."

She really was very old. The sun was setting, and the red rays made her skin seem transparent. I took her dry, warm hand and stood by her for a moment. Like her neighbors, her qualities were of the salt of the earth; she had bequeathed us the strength necessary to endure and which made us intolerable.

"There are so many things I want to ask you," I said.

My grandmother sighed, and her eyes wandered down toward the river. "I've seen a great deal," she said. Her smile had faded; the lines of her face were resigned.

"Can't you tell me anything?"

After a time she shook her head slightly. "You'll be all right, Juley."

The cottonwood leaves stirred. My grandmother still looked out toward the water; that current had been running a long time. In her place I began to see another figure, my lover's, sitting with his face as contorted as his knotted fists, the way he sat the day he told me he was afraid of me.

—*I'm so in awe of you, Juley, he had said, and at last, mumbling, you make me feel so inadequate*—

—*But I want you!*

—*Oh, I've had my fantasies of running away with you somewhere, but*—

And I had been left crying to myself, *but I don't mean to make you in awe of me, I love you*—

—*They say the old lady drove him to it.*

And I saw one more scene, one I had forgotten, another aftermath of recriminations in the night. My grandmother's sudden exclamation, a match scratching in the dark. I a child of nine or so, staying with my grandparents so I could go to school, waking suddenly and sitting up in my cot.

—*David, for pity's sake! Come back here!*

—*No, no, Juley!* This not to the Juley who was quaking in her nightgown, bare feet already on the cold floor, but to the other Juley, my grandmother.

—David!

The screen door slammed. I ran across the floor and out into the night; it must have been late fall. No snow yet, but cold air. I saw that one white figure had reached the yard fence while the second hurried in pursuit. The first figure climbed the fence with ease and loped off across the neighboring pasture.

—David! The second figure moved more awkwardly, had to stop for the gate. It was losing ground. Both heads were gray in the moonlight. The first figure shouted back a child's taunt.

—You can't catch me, Juley!

I could remember no further. The sun had gone down, and the air from the river was cold. My grandmother's eyes had closed; her breathing was shallow.

"Are you cold, Grandmother?"

She shook her head slightly.

"I'm leaving in the morning, Grandmother."

A slight nod. Then her eyes opened again, and she repeated, "You'll be all right, Juley."

Stall Warning

"Take her up to six thousand feet," I tell her, and she gives me that tight look as if I'd tell her to crash while I'm for chrissake sitting in the right seat of the plane alongside of her. But after swallowing she says,

"Full throttle?"

"You want to climb, don't you?" I says.

And blushing because she now remembers what I told her last week, she shoves in the throttle and hauls back on the wheel, too goddamn heavy-handed of course but they all are at first, and the Chickenhawk roars upstairs while the layers of blue fall off behind us. At this altitude in the Chickenhawk, which is my name for the Cessna 172 because it's so slow though it's a good plane don't get me wrong and a forgiving plane but a slow bitch, you lose all sense of speed so it seems like you're hanging up here out of the reach of gravity and oh shit it's pretty. Hell I guess I thought after last week it'd look different up here which shows what your mind can do to you.

She lets the altimeter reach six thousand feet before she tries to level off, so naturally we're at sixty-five hundred before she notices it, and when she does she overcorrects by shoving the nose down.

"Jesuschrist!" I yell at her, "You can't manhandle a plane like that! You got to relax! Let up! Look what you're doing! Shit, you just lost another two hundred feet. Remember what I told you last week? Keep your eyes outside the plane and not on the instrument panel, because you're not an instrument pilot and you can't read them instruments yet. You just watch that strip of horizon over the cowling. Remember what I told you? As long as that strip of horizon stays constant your altitude stays constant. Fifty feet variance in altitude either way is all they allow you on the check ride."

She's flustered now and red in the face but she's figured out how

to level out at five thousand feet and hold it. "That's better," I tell
her, and it is better. Shit, she's no worse than any other student
pilot. And she gives a little sigh, all grateful because I've let up on
her for the moment and because she's got no idea what's in store
for her next.

"Okay. You remember how I told you to trim for slow flight?"

No, she doesn't. Embarrassed, she starts to explain something
over the roar of the engine but thinks better of it because she can't
talk and fly at the same time.

"Remember? If you want slow flight you bring the nose up. If
you want speed you push the nose down. If you want to climb,
you add throttle."

She nods.

"Shit, you got to more than remember!" All of a sudden my
hands are shaking like I was afraid was going to happen. "You got
to know it so good—you got to practice it till it seems like the
natural thing to do, which it ain't. The natural thing to do when
you lose altitude is pull the nose up, which you can't never do,
because it'll kill you." And I didn't mean to say that but Terry you
fucking son of a bitch I hope you're listening. "Speed means nose
down, and slow flight means nose up, and throttle is to climb, and
you got to make that be natural for you. Okay. You remember
how to trim? Trim for forty miles an hour."

I lean back against the door with my hands in my pockets while
she scowls and talks to herself and finally works out what it is she
has to do, which is bring the nose up gradual and ease back on the
throttle until we're hanging up there over the practice area on our
backs with the tail underneath us and the cowling blotting out
everything but blue sky and the sun on the windshield. After her
arm starts to ache from holding the nose up, she remembers the
trim and spins it back, overcorrecting at first and then getting it just
right. Hell, she ain't going to be too bad. If she keeps flying.

But in spite of myself I have to laugh at her. "No reason why you
have to choke that wheel to death."

She stares at her hand like she's never seen it before. Her
knuckles are white and wet from the death grip she's got on the

wheel until, forcing a smile when I laugh at her again, she pries her fingers loose and flexes them.

"You're doing all right. What you got to get over is fighting the airplane. That's half your trouble right now. Ease up! You're all the time trying too hard. Hell with the plane, it'll damn near fly itself if you give it a chance. See there? You're maintaining altitude just fine now you ain't thinking about it."

She looks at the altimeter and immediately she drops fifty feet and overcorrects. I wait until she's back at six thousand feet and steady. This time her smile isn't forced. She's getting the idea.

"It's harder for a woman. Anything mechanical is," I say to cheer her up, but all I get for it is a dirty look. Hell, I won't argue about it, but I've taught a lot of women to fly and the only difference between them and her is I knew why they wanted to learn but I got no idea what she's after. A woman student pilot is usually some private pilot's wife who's been flying around the country with him and has figured out what would happen if she was along with him the day he had a fatal heart attack at maybe twelve thousand feet. This girl I don't know. She's not married and I know she had to borrow the money for the lessons. But she goes at it like her life depended on it.

"Okay, put your carb heat on."

She does it without asking why, so I break the news. "We're gonna practice some stalls now, and the first thing you always want to do before you do stalls is put on the carb heat and make sure there's no ice in the carburetor."

She's looking at me now and not at what she's doing, and she's all white around the mouth, but the worst thing that's going to happen to her is she may get airsick and have to puke in front of me. But hell, she's a big girl.

"Did you read about stalls like I told you to?"

She nods.

"Okay, what causes a stall?"

"Slow speed?" she yells over the roar.

"That's part of it, but remember what I told you about lift?"

She nods with her eyes on me, all wide and glassy like she might change her mind about what she read if I shake my head. "It's the lift under the wings that keeps you flying. The steeper your angle of attack, the less lift you got to keep you flying. You get past a certain angle and she quits flying on you."

She's dry-mouthed now and ready to quit herself, except there's no way she can get out at six thousand feet, and she don't know which is worse, looking at me or looking at the airspeed indicator.

"It's all gravity in the long run, honey, it's all gravity. And we practice stalls now so if you ever stall by accident, your body'll do the right thing, because your mind it won't stand a chance. I know you don't like it, but it's not dangerous as long as you keep your mind on flying, so quit looking so sick. You think I'd be up here if I thought we were gonna crash? Okay. I want you to keep coming back with that wheel. Bring that nose farther and farther back until first the stall warning comes on and then you'll feel the plane give a little lurch under you. That's how you know she's stalled. Then you push the nose down to recover and at the same time you give her full throttle. You got that? You push *down* even though your instinct's gonna tell you to pull up, and then you come in with full throttle. Okay?"

She ain't liking it at all, but mouth tight she starts to drag back on the wheel, and right away I see she's got the problem a lot of woman pilots have and that's not enough left-arm muscle. She's got her right hand on the throttle where it belongs and with her left hand she's hauling back on the wheel, getting red-faced now and squirming around in her seat to try and get some leverage. We're on our backs again with nothing in front of us but cowling and clouds, and at last the stall warning starts to howl. You can't hear nothing but the stall warning once it starts, and she panics and drops the nose. The stall warning quits and I yell, "Come on! Pull! Stall her out!"

She pulls like hell and the stall warning starts in to screeching again, rackety goddamn thing and *it must have been the last thing Terry ever heard* and fuck I got to keep my mind off that. "Pull!"

She's grinding her teeth now and pulling with her eyes popped out of her face, but shit she's not a very big girl to start with and she just ain't got the muscle. Finally I take hold of the control on my side and lean back until the Chickenhawk gives a little flutter like she's been shot dead in the air. "You feel that?"

The goddamn stall warning is screeching like a banshee all the time, but I'll be go to hell but she pushes the nose down and adds throttle without looking at me to see if she's doing the right thing. The next minute the windshield is full of pasture and summer-fallow coming at us at two hundred miles an hour. Then it's clouds again and a steady horizon and damned if she ain't leveled the old Chickenhawk out without losing more than a couple hundred feet of altitude. Now that everything is under control from her point of view she does look at me, white in the face and wet and limp, and I tell her, "Okay, do it again."

She whimpers but she starts pulling back, and I wonder all over again why she's so set on learning to fly. It ain't just since she's had a lesson, either. I could tell it the day I talked to her on the telephone the first time. And shit I guess it's a good thing I went ahead and gave her a lesson last week because I sure the hell wouldn't have the heart to start a new pupil this week. Oh eventually, I know, give me a week or two and it'll be like nothing ever happened, but I wouldn't have minded putting her off today. Because she's new, that's the only reason. I should have had one of the guys with me this first time because the guys mostly know what happened and knew him and feel the same way I do and I guess that's what makes the difference and *oh shit Terry of all the stupid goddamn fucking things you could have done* and here I am letting my mind run on it again while she's actually gritted her teeth and damn near pulled the Chickenhawk back into a stall all by herself. At the last minute I give her a little help and the Chickenhawk lurches, we're over the top and falling fields rushing at us again and she's pushing the nose down and adding full throttle. Not quite such a smooth recovery this time. Funny how often the first try is the best try for a long time. I got to keep my mind on my work, that's for sure. "Okay, do it again."

She sighs and I take a look at her because she's had a workout, all right. I remember what it feels like. Your blood turns to water you're so scared and the spit rises out of your mouth just before you get sick except you can't get sick, your guts are still a thouand feet above you, and it's happening too fast anyway, all over in less time than it takes to tell about it. What you realize only later is, there was nothing to be scared about. Just an exercise the instructor was making you practice. Only once or twice since I first soloed I've felt the same way, and once was flying through that electrical storm a year ago. No reason to be scared most of the time. It's the safest way to go as long as you don't make a mistake, but I know what it feels like in that split second you got to feel anything in and *I got to quit thinking about it.*

"Listen," I tell her to distract myself, "don't look so goddamned scared. Don't you know a stall's nothing to be scared of? Do you think I'd tell you to crash? Listen now—hey, does it bother you when I yell at you?"

"Yes," she says. "No," she adds quickly.

"I yell so's to get through to you. I know you're trying to think about everything at once, but you also got to act in a hurry and when I yell it eventually gets through. Hell, I yell at the men, too." Terry told me after the first couple lessons he was ready to punch me out for it. "Because it's the only way you're gonna learn, right? Now look. These stalls ain't dangerous. It's not knowing what to do that's dangerous. Because there's nothing dangerous about flying unless you make a mistake. Try it again."

She leans back on the wheel like a good girl, but she's too tired.

"Come on, show some muscle," I urge, but she can't, so I go on talking to give her a chance to rest.

"No, these stalls ain't dangerous. We come way up here to practice so you got plenty of airspace to recover in. It's a low altitude stall you got to watch."

She gives me a quick look, picking up on something, I don't know what. Oh shit. "All pilots practice stalls. It's the first thing you do in a new plane. You take her up to altitude and check out where she stalls. Look here." I draw back on the right seat control, treading on the left rudder at the same time to keep us steady against the torque of the propellor, which is another thing she's having trouble doing, and bring us way back with the nose lifting all the time into the clear blue and the cirrus streaks twenty thousand feet above us until at last she lurches and falters and I push the nose down and recover. Lurches push the nose down recover lurches push the nose down recover. Three stalls in less than a minute. "See, there's nothing to it. No big deal as long as you don't make a mistake."

"That's what I'm scared of," she yells over the engine noise.

"What? Making a mistake?"

She nods, then shoots me that quick embarrassed look of hers. "That pilot—the one that was killed last week," she shouts. "The guys were talking about him. They said he just made a dumb mistake."

All I can say is, "It was dumb, all right."

"You knew him, then?"

"I taught him to fly."

She looks stricken. I hear my own voice hurrying to make it all right: "Which is why you practice these goddamn stalls, so you won't forget and do like he done, which was to come in over the goddamn knoll alongside the Turner airstrip like he had a hundred times only this time he forgot to watch his airspeed—" while all the time my mind is saying he was as good a student pilot as I ever had, he was as good a pilot as I am, so what do you think you're doing up here telling some poor little bitch she's safe so long as she don't make a mistake? Let somebody that still thinks he knows what he's talking about give flying lessons.

The sun is burning through the windshield and I'm breaking into a sweat, but at six thousand feet there ain't no way out but straight down. Give me time, I tell myself like I've been telling myself all week. Give me time and I'll be the same as I ever was.

To keep from listening to any more of my own lies, I'm about to tell her to head for the airport and land this crate when without any warning something like a bucket of goddamn bricks gets dropped on my stomach and I can't breathe and *Jesus I got to get out of here* except there ain't nothing between me and all of screaming space but a piece of glass and a strip of cowling and a two-inch-wide safety belt that this minute is stretching like a piece of chewing gum as the cockpit spins.

The plane ain't in a spin. Part of me knows she's flying along level and not even knowing anything's wrong with me while the rest of me is still trying to get my breath back. It's the other part of me that finally pulls me out of it.

Some way I work up the spit to use my voice. "Okay," I hear myself croak, "try one more stall and then we'll head in. Your hour'll be up by the time we get on the ground." And she leans back, really relaxed now and feeling good because the lesson's just about over and because she don't know this one more stall is for me and not for her.

Jesus I ain't never been through nothing like that minute or two there. Flying through that lightning storm was nothing.

She glances over and I wonder if she sees two of me. No she don't. Now that she's decided there ain't nothing to be scared of, she's bringing the nose back just as steady as an old hand. She don't even wince when the stall warning comes howling on, and she gives it the last ounce all by herself, drawing the nose back until the Chickenhawk flutters and stalls. It's me that's sweating and fighting with myself not to reach out and push the nose down with the right-hand control and add power and head for the airport, God anything to get on the ground in a hurry. Except if I ever did that I know I'd never go up again.

Shit, she's doing it. She's pushing the nose down, adding power and leveling out as the fields advance and recede below us, and she's turning to me, face glowing because she knows she did it right.

"You think you can find the airport from here?" I croak.

I must sound all right, though, because she looks around and points east. She's kept her directions straight.

"Okay, let's take her in."

She banks and heads east like she'd been flying a year instead of a week, and I lean back and think about sitting still. I'm okay. I'm okay. What a hell of a thing to happen, is all. But I'm better now. I can act normal.

"I been meaning to ask you," I yell, "how come you want to learn to fly?"

She looks at me blank, like why does there have to be a reason for it? Or maybe what's wrong with him? But I must be doing a good job of acting normal, because her eyes clear up and she yells back,

"I guess I thought if I learned to fly, I could do anything."

I never thought of that as a reason, but thinking about it helps get my mind back on the track. Sure, all that's the matter with me is my mind jumped the tracks. I sure the hell hope I ain't been off the track all along and didn't just get a minute's glimpse of the way it really is. But I'm okay, I'm okay, and in five minutes we'll be on the ground. Don't want to think about the ground. Think about her. So what's she doing, thinking she can learn to fly and learn to do anything? Maybe she's as bad as I am and has to do one more stall to keep from losing it.

"So how do you like it now?" I yell.

Damned if her eyes don't light up in spite of the stalls and she yells back, "Great! It's like—" she's thinking it over—"like it's my life I'm on top of!"

Yes, and she's flying all easy and relaxed now, not a care in the world, which she'll have to unlearn *can't never get cocky, I told him once. I don't remember why because he never was.*

"Just remember! You got to keep your mind on what you're doing. These airplanes are built safe, the new ones anyway. They got double electrical systems and 100-hour overhauls and the works and hell, like I say, the plane will almost fly itself if you let it, but you always got to have your mind on it. You can't never get cocky."

She looks at me, only half hearing what I'm saying, because the sun is too bright up here and the sky too blue for anything to happen. And my hands start to shake again.

"You just told me not to be scared," she argues.

"That's right, except there's a time to be scared and that's when it feels too safe. When you get to sitting up here feeling fine and feeling like that ground down there ain't real, that's when you need to be scared, because you ain't never out of the reach of gravity, honey."

She sighs, not following it all. "It's the not making a mistake that worries me," she says. "I mean, to err is human, you know?"

Yeah, I know. But at least I can stop talking if I can't stop think-ing, because we've got the airport in sight and she can't listen to me and think about her pre-landing check at the same time.

"Well?" I bark when she does nothing, and she gives me a funny look. I can tell she's forgotten what to do, so I start calling out the checklist.

"Carb heat. You don't still have it on, do you? No, you don't. Good. Trim. Tab. Throttle. Radio. Call the unicom on your base leg even though they probably won't answer after all the fussing they did to get that unicom center. Trim for eighty, that's your ap-proach speed. You've got time now to look for other aircraft. They're supposed to call in just like you do, but sometimes they forget and you're just as dead when it's their fault. That's right, check your altimeter as you turn downwind. Don't let it get below 3000 yet. Do you remember how high we are above sea level?"

No, of course she don't. She's holding the mike and trying to remember our call letters and adjust the trim tab at the same time and remember what altitude she's supposed to be when she turns for final.

"Okay, you got another chance just before you turn final to check for other aircraft, and look there! There comes Louie in his spray plane. That son of a bitch has a full set of radios in that outfit, but you think he can be bothered to use them? No, he just comes barreling in like he was the only plane in the sky. That's right, you let him go ahead and land. You're fine, but that's why you've al-ways got to watch out. Okay now. Turn final. Turn *turn* now god-damn it! Keep your corner nice and square *square* not rounded off like that. See, now you got to jockey around to get your approach straight. You can't come in for a landing all screwed around sideways. Straighten her out! Okay, that's better watch your al-titude you'll never make the runway if you don't give her a little power *power* power goddamn it!"

Terry coming in for a landing and that goddamn little knoll just east of the approach at the Turner airstrip and they said afterward he'd tried to get out of his seatbelt oh fuck he just came in too slow was all forgot about his airspeed forgot about that knoll wasn't thinking about what he was doing it only takes once. To make mistakes is human, all right.

"Goddamn it, watch your airspeed! Jesuschrist you're close to stall speed. Listen, you want to stall at this altitude? That's what you've got to be scared of. You can't let your speed drop at this altitude. Okay, give her power. Okay, now you see you got the runway made, and you can cut back and—okay, now, just let the airspeed bleed off. Let her settle down gradual. No, no, hold her off no don't jerk her up like that, you'll stall her out! That's better. Let her settle. Okay, start your flare, but keep holding the nose off. That's right. Let all that airspeed bleed away. *Hold the nose off. Pull, damn it! Pull! Hold the nose off!*"

Hell, she just ain't strong enough. She's pulling for all she's worth.

"Hold the nose off," I bellow, and bump, bump, the tail comes down, and we bounce fifty feet and settle down again, and this time she manages to hold the nose off and we're on the runway, slowing down. I take over, stepping on the disc brakes to slow us down before we get to the last turnoff because I don't want to end up on the far end of the runway and have to taxi all the way back again.

And I glance over at her now. She's looking a little sick, but hell, she didn't do too bad for her second time in the air. You have to remember it's only her second time.

"Hell, you landed her," I tell her as I lean on the right rudder and turn off on the access pavement. She brightens right up. "I guess I'm going to learn to fly after all!"

"Sure you are. You just got to learn to keep control of the airplane."

What I want to tell her is you ain't never in control, you only think you are. We've taxied up in front of the administration building by now and she's sitting there with her hair stringing in her face, all sweaty, and hoping I'll say something. Tell her something. Shit, what can I say? That being on top is not all she thinks it's going to be and that to make mistakes is human and that the only way out is straight down? Or that I'll feel better next week? Because what else is there to do?

"You did fine," I tell her.

Her face is shining. "I'll be back next week," she says. "You got me hooked on it, all right. I'm going to learn to fly!"

"That's good," I tell her. Because what else is there? We get out of the plane and walk to the administration building, legs shaky the way they always are on solid earth, and through the door into the office where another kid is waiting for a flying lesson, kinda scared and kinda excited.

"I'll be right with you," I tell him, "as soon as I log her hour."

Bare Trees

The noise of the weekend crowd in the Jubilee Bar had risen to the blur of fever, the electronics of the jukebox no longer distinguishable from human tones, and faces and all lights becoming one. Junie Sweet stirred in confusion. She couldn't see Verna. The barstool dug into her buttocks and hurt her, but there was nowhere else for her to sit, and now she had to pee.

Junie lifted one hand carefully and steadied herself against the bar. Slowly, so her brain wouldn't start to spin, she turned her head and looked at the wallboard partition that hid the corridor to the ladies' room. Sooner or later she would have to get off the barstool and go. Her mind anticipated the trip, taking her out of the hot roaring darkness and into the brightly lighted corridor that was so narrow she had to turn sideways to squeeze herself through it. Then there would be the sour smell of the ladies' room and the ordeal of backing into the stall, her pants already around her ankles because there wouldn't be room to get them down once she was in there—and likely some lady combing her hair and ready to bitch her out for what she couldn't help—but at last the delicious relief of the emptying bladder. She had to go so bad she could taste it. But she wouldn't go yet. She'd put it off as long as she could.

Junie fumbled back to face the bar and found her glass with what was left of her beer. Every swallow was an ill-afforded luxury, easing her brain as it intensified the burning of her bladder.

She drained her glass and stared at it. Now her beer was all gone. Verna must be somewhere. Carefully Junie swivelled her head to search the jammed and yelping crowd in the semi-darkness. She and Verna had come in together, and sometimes one of Verna's boyfriends would buy a beer for Verna's cousin.

"You gonna have another one or not?"

Junie squinted, but the light behind the bar was too intense and she could not make out the face of the barmaid although she knew she must be standing in front of her. But she did know she either must buy another beer or move.

"Another one," she mumbled.

"Let's see your sixty-five cents."

Her ears throbbed with the refusal but she had expected no better. Some people could order a drink and it would arrive without question, but the barmaids all knew who to serve. They would let Billy order drinks. He had his pension money, and he would buy for her tonight if he were downtown, but Billy went to bed early. Junie could always go up to his room and get a couple dollars—without asking leave, her mind wandered out of the Jubilee and across the street, flitting up the bare stairs in the rear of the hotel and hovering outside the second door on the third floor like a will-o'-the-wisp teasing the dull body that could not keep up with it. She could visualize the door that would open and the bright street colors that would spill through the window overlooking First Street. She could pick out Billy's shallow outline in the bed. Billy was easy to rouse. "Junie?" Once he had recognized her, he would pick his pants up off the floor, knowing how hard it was for her to stoop, and rummage for what he had to give her, dimes and quarters, and not even ask her to do anything unless she felt like it. He knew she wouldn't forget. She could imagine all this, but she still sat in the Jubilee with the cold street and the stairs between her and Billy.

And Verna. Verna had to be someplace, and Junie didn't like to leave without Verna even if she knew Billy wouldn't expect her to stay.

"Okay, okay! Either pay or get off the pot. You've had plenty of time."

Junie slid to the floor, steadying herself to get her bearings and clamping her sphincter against the pressure of her bladder. She'd better get to the pot while she could and look for Verna later.

"—never saw such a bastard for luck! You know how many coyotes he shot?" somebody bawled in her ear.

"What?" Junie mumbled trying to make out the face next to hers. Gradually she saw that it was not a face at all, but the back of

a head turned toward another man farther down the bar. "They're talking about hunting," she told herself. "Coyote hunting," she mumbled out loud, and heard somebody squeal her name:
   "Swe-ee-t! Swee-ee-t!"
   Verna got mad when they pig-squealed at Junie. Maybe Verna had gone somewhere. Carefully Junie began to walk toward the corridor, although she had to find a way around the tables and chairs and bodies with eyes that glittered in the green gleam of the jukebox and mouths that bared their teeth and roared.

   Back of the wallboard partition was even worse, because a bare light bulb in the ceiling turned everything before her eyes into black spinning stars. She had to squint her eyes and hold onto the wall until the stars subsided and she could control her stomach and open her eyes to see the cracked yellow tile and the plywood door on a spring.

   Once in the room she had to begin the tedious process of getting her pants down. All physical movement for Junie had to be calculated. Sometimes, after a habit she had begun as a child, she would mutter instructions to herself. To tie her shoe, she always told herself how far to stand behind one chair so she could prop her foot on a rung while she steadied herself on the back of another chair until she could lean around the barrier of her stomach and titties to reach her shoelaces without losing her balance. The exercise and the anxiety always left her short of breath. When she could get them, she liked sloppy shoes she could stuff her feet into without bending. Stretch pants were okay; the stretch shirts Mrs. Werner kept leaving in the box for her and that had to be pulled over her head were a suffocating nightmare.

   "Pull 'em part-way down in front," she mumbled. "And part-way down in back. Then Junie's pants be okay. Now back up," she told herself. "You be okay."

   As she hobbled backward with her pants around her knees, she felt the plywood walls on both sides of the stall rasp at the polyester fabric of her blouse. When she thought she was close enough, she began to squirm downward. The rough grain of the wood raised tufts of synthetic thread from her blouse and compressed her bare thighs as gradually she lowered herself to a sitting position and felt the porcelain ring under her. She sighed with relief and let go her stream.

"Junie's okay," she whispered, just as Gumma used to. "Junie's a good girl."

The warmth of her emptying bladder comforted her. Sometimes it was bad to recall Gumma, always bad to think much about how Gumma had been, but often good to let the old warm feelings flow back. Junie twisted one arm forward out of the vise of the plywood walls and her own sides until she could pat herself, gently, on her own shoulder, one-two-three pats just as if it was Gumma's hand. The fingers warm and firm against her shoulder and the warm friendly smell of her own urine—Junie held her fist against her nose and breathed flesh and blood and comfort. Gumma had kept quilts on the bed to rub and smell. Even better to hold against her nose now than her own fist was Billy's quilt with its old-man smell. She was glad of Billy. It didn't make her cry to think of Billy's face the way it did when she thought of how Gumma's wrinkles had looked and how whiskers had sprouted above her lip and out of her mole. Suddenly Junie was feeling very bad.

"Junie's a good girl," she whispered, and thought desperately of Billy.

Junie started as the door was jerked open and somebody, she couldn't tell who from where she sat in the stall, lurched through. Her hands twitched at her pants, but she was trapped. Getting off the pot and twisting out of the stall was an agonizing process that made getting into it seem ordinary. She could not reach around behind herself to flush the toilet, and she could not escape to the bar and disassociate herself from her mess before she would get bitched out for being a stinking dirty Geeta.

The footsteps stopped in front of her. Junie tilted back her head and squinted against the hundred-watt light bulb set over the sink. Relief overwhelmed her as the other woman's features cleared.

"Verna," she grinned.

Verna bent double at the waist, her gums bared to the gaps in her molars, and squealed at her cousin. Verna's thighs were match-sticks, her knees indecent juttings under her levis. The flesh of her arms barely enclosed the bones. Always Verna had been a skeleton, in spite of Gumma—*jess can't fill that kid up, never seen such a one*—and now she had only the start of a pot belly and a roll around the waist to show for all her beer. It was as though, in spite of all Gumma could do, one little girl starved and shrank upon her bones while the other little girl waxed on her nourishment and grew and swelled into an embarrassment of love that would not leave off. Gumma fed them both on hot cakes and Karo syrup. One little girl flourished and grew, overblossomed and unfolded and spread. The other little girl gained nothing. Her shanks were blue. She felt the cold easily. At night she had to crowd for warmth against the flesh of her cousin. Junie encompassed her when she could, for it hurt her to see the sharp points of Verna's bones.

"Junie!" howled Verna, leaning on the stall. Her rigid upswept hair leaned with her, only denting slightly when it bumped against the plywood. Junie opened her mouth to tell Verna to sit down on the floor and she would come and hold her as soon as she could wrench herself free of the stall. But then Verna got her bearings, and her expression became absorbed. "Jesus but I gotta pee!" she hissed.

Junie heard her cousin's boot heels clatter into the other stall. She felt relieved. In a moment she would squirm out of the stall and pull her pants back up and tell Verna she was going up to Billy's. Unless Verna wanted her to stay. But Verna looked as if she was okay.

Junie sighed. Part of her mind directed her, as it always had to, through her struggle to free her flesh from the constrictions of the world around her. But the better part of her mind had flitted back across the street to the rear stairs of the hotel, even stopping and waiting on the landing for her to catch her breath as she always did. The stairs always were cold, though not as cold as the street, and her breath would whiten in great puffs that gradually ebbed only to puff out again as she began, one step at a time like a child, to ascend the last flight.

Without asking leave, her mind leaped ahead to Billy.

"Hahn?" he would gasp, startled out of his sleep no matter how carefully she turned the doorknob he had left unlocked for her.

The blank scared look in his eyes during the moment it always took him to recognize her was the only part she hated. Her eyes had learned to look away, but her mind was not so considerate.

Holding her breath, Junie twisted her shoulders twice, three times, and wrenched herself out of the stall. She could feel her grateful flesh expand in every direction as she let out her breath. Bending carefully to keep her head from swimming and upsetting her balance, she reached for her pants around the familiar ache of flesh caught in the vise of thighs and shoulders.

"Junie!" wept Verna.

Bent double and still holding her pants, Junie shuffled around until she could look into the stall. Verna was leaning back against the pot, her face yellow.

"Wassa matter?"

"I can't get up."

Out of habit Junie hauled at her pants, getting them up as far as her crotch before straightening and catching her breath for the final haul. But her eyes were on Verna. Verna was crying, her face twisted into lines as deep as scars in the glare of the light bulb.

Junie tried to think. "You sick?" she asked.

"My legs j-jess quit on me."

Verna's legs, bare to the calves where her levis had bunched on her boottops, did look like pitiful sticks to hold up even skinny Verna.

"You gonna be okay," Junie promised while she tried to think of something. She gave her pants the final hitch over her abdomen and straightened herself. She wanted to see Billy badly, but that would have to be after awhile. "After awhile," she mumbled to herself.

"Junie!"

"I'm gonna give you a hand," Junie reassured her. Carefully she positioned herself in front of Verna's stall, sideways so she could reach her arm as far as she could. But there was no answering handclasp.

Slowly Junie turned her head and peered over the soft mountain of her shoulder. Her own hand was outstretched, but Verna's hung limp.

"Reach!" she commanded.

"I can't," sobbed Verna. "My arms, they don't want to work neither."

Junie could think of nothing else to do. She was too big to move her arms if she got inside the stall with Verna, and yet, stretch as she might, she could not reach her from without. She sighed. Verna still was crying.

"Don't cry. I'm gonna come and get you."

Junie shuffled in a half-circle to stand facing the stall. With her arms outstretched, she lurched hard against the stall to force herself forward a step or two and get hold of Verna under her armpits. The constriction was so great that Junie hardly could breathe.

"Okay," she gasped. "I got you, honey."

With another lurch she forced her arms upward and felt Verna fall against her breasts. "Okay!" she managed to gasp again and heaved herself backward as hard as she could.

Like a cork escaping a bottle, they popped out of the stall and, carried by the momentum of Junie's weight, across the three steps between the stall and the sink where they came to rest violently, arms around each other. Junie could feel Verna's dry sobs even as she herself wheezed desperately to get her breath. "Ho-hokay!" she panted. "You hokay now!"

Verna really was okay. Extricating her from the stall somehow had restored feeling to her arms and legs. She shook free from Junie's enveloping flesh and giggled.

"Pop!" she crowed, waving her sticks of arms.

Junie still was wheezing too hard to laugh, but she was relieved. She pushed herself up from the sink, which had begun to creak against the wall, and smiled. Verna was okay and Junie could leave her and go up to Billy's.

For just a moment the thought of the three flights of stairs at the hotel after so much exertion was overwhelming. Could she manage so much? Could she even get across the street? For she seemed to have spent far more breath than she had, though she had not calculated the price of Verna's need, and now her lungs burned and ached.

But like a reward came a vision of the darkened room, the

colored pools of light that fell through the hotel's lace curtains, and the musky smell and the dry paper feel of Billy's elderly shanks as she bent to bury her face in his groin. She never had felt so lucky to have Billy.

"Pop!" shrilled Verna. She had drawn up her levis and buckled her wide tooled belt with the silver rodeo trophy buckle John Thumb had given her. She capered, eyes sparkling.

"Pop pop," Junie tried to respond. But talking was an effort. She leaned cautiously back against the sink and listened to the rasp of her own breathing.

"Come on, honey," Verna urged. "Gotta drink up."

"I ain't got no more money," Junie gasped. She knew Mrs. Werner would have a fit if she could see her now. *Have you been taking your shots? Young lady, do you know what will happen to you if you go on drinking beer and don't take your insulin?*

But Verna was tugging at her. "These guys out there, they don't care, they buy you a beer. Okay?"

Junie allowed herself to be tugged. Her bulk was her ally now, for even Verna could not hurry that huge body through the narrow corridor. Even so, the effort to move and breathe at the same time was overwhelming. "Wait!" she bleated.

But she was relieved to get out of the glare of the light bulb in the corridor and into the protection of the darkened barroom. Even here the light was too bright, glowing up from the jukebox and down from the beer signs to expose all the forms in the shadows and the eyes and the ruffs and the snarling masks. Junie quailed. Only Verna's persistent fingers on her wrist were a link with her own kind.

Verna, still none too steady, dragged Junie to a table by the jukebox. Junie watched as Verna's face turned green in its glow.

"Verna! There she is! Atta baby!"

"Wassa matter, honey, you fall in?"

Junie could not make out their faces in the dark or even be sure how many of them were around the table, but their eyes and teeth flashed greenish as the song on the jukebox changed to a ballad. Junie's head was clearing as at last she got her wind, and she knew she needed another beer to dull what she saw. If only Verna could get them to buy her one.

"*Swe-ee-t! Swe-ee-t!*"

"Shut up, you son of a bitch!" Verna aimed a kick into the dark, her eyes bulging.

A hand grabbed her wrist. "Don't you call me no names, you goddamn fucking Geeta bitch!"

"Aw, back off. She just needs another beer, is all. Don't you, Verna?"

Beers were arriving on a tray from the bar. Junie licked her lips. There was one for her. She held the cool wet glass in her fingers. She got the first fast gulp down and saw the eyes and fangs recede into shadowy faces. She drained the bottle.

She felt better. Verna was on somebody's lap, shrieking and pulling his blond hair, but Junie remained standing with her stomach thrust forward and her feet spread apart to equalize her weight. It was more comfortable than trying to squat on one of the cruel metal chairs. Her breathing had evened, and her lungs only ached if she drew a trifle too hard against them. She even had another beer. This one she could afford to sip slowly. Her eyes dwelt on Verna.

The ballad ended with a silence as abrupt as a blow. Shouts rose from the gloom.

"What the hell, nobody got money for that bitch?"

"Hey, Dee! Shove some change up that thing!"

"You know how many coyotes that son of a bitch has shot this winter?" said the blond man, pulling away from Verna.

"Listen," another man interrupted. "My dad used to tell me about a fellow, years ago, that hunted coyotes with a pair of rat terriers. A male and a female. He'd send the terriers down a coyote den to bring the pups out. He needed the scalps for the bounty, of course. Well, the old male dog would go down into a den and kill the pups and fetch them out one at a time, dead. But the female would carry the pups out alive and start to lick them. Animals sure can be human."

"You call that human?"

Junie thought more shapes had crowded around. When she was jostled she swung her head nervously, for her balance was so easily upset she had to be on her guard. Even through the beer fumes she caught the alien scent of oil and smoke and young males. They all were shouting.

"—out at Smithville they got a live band—"

"—less go—"

"Come on, Junie," said Verna.

"No, shit, we ain't taking her."

Junie tried to make out Verna's face. "I want to go see Billy," she tried to explain. "I been wanting him."

A chorus of voices swelled and broke around her, some in her ears, some at a distance, everyone shouting and yet no one answering.

"Swe-ee-t! Swe-ee-t!"

"You shut the hell up, you hear? And I ain't going noplace without her, you hear that?"

"I been wanting Billy," Junie whimpered, trying to make Verna hear her. But then Verna turned from the core of the uproar so Junie could see her face and recognize the fear that gripped the lines of Verna's mouth and brought beads to the surface of her lips. *Oh Verna let's get out of here and go find Gumma. Out on the hill behind the house it's warm and only thing to watch where you step is ticks and snakes and there's Gumma, Gumma to put us under the big quilt and oh Verna don't be cold.* She knew she could not leave Verna. Billy was a secret center of warmth for Junie, but Junie was all the center Verna had.

"Listen, you guys get the hell out of here," ordered the barmaid. "There's decent people wants to enjoy themselves without listening to your foul mouths."

Verna was clutching at Junie's wrist. Her fingers were cold. Junie's flesh crawled under the chill of Verna's bones. "Okay," she whispered. "Okay."

Now they were out of the bar and standing on the sidewalk in the wind that usually went down after dark but tonight was whining against the brick walls and the locked parked cars and through

Junie's coat to remind her of something she had forgotten, like a shred of a dream that she couldn't quite bring back to mind. The cement felt insubstantial under her feet. Her center of gravity swayed and returned in a full circle. She wanted to look across the street to Billy's window, even though she knew there would be no light, but the wind blew dirt into her face.

A car door yawned open. In the yellow ceiling light she saw a grinning fox mask, eyes and teeth and ear tufts in a chiaroscuro of dark and light, mounted upon a man's torso and shoulders in the deepest corner of the back seat. The mouth peeled back in a grin, the arms outstretched. She felt herself being pushed toward them. Once her bulk was moving downward there was no stopping.

Another hard body was wedging itself in behind her, legs stiffening against the floor to get enough clearance to slam the door. The scent of young males in the close space was pervasive. Verna's head, a shiny black disc of hair, protruded above the middle of the front seat. Junie heard Verna's giggle and thought she must be all right. Verna always was all right—no, Verna never was all right—but she was all right with the young men. Junie sighed and let her folds relax into all the crevices left between the men on either side of her. They were plastered against the windows by her bulk.

"Jesuschrist there's hardly room to breathe back here!"

Now the bar lights were streaming past the windshield, and the headlights were opening into darkness. Junie saw the shadow of the grain elevator as they crossed the railroad tracks and turned out on the highway. Someone in the front seat, a one-dimensional figure in a black nylon jacket, was breaking cans of beer out of a cardboard container and passing them over the seat. Foam slopped over and wet her knee, but Junie could not get a hand free to take a can. In the front seat Verna had gotten hers and was trying to drink.

A yelp from the young man in the black jacket—"Fuck, I'm soaked!" and Verna ki-yied as he sent her lurching against the driver with a backhand slap. Suddenly the headlights were sweeping wildly across fence posts and bleached grass instead of open highway. The car was full of shouts—"Holy shit, we're in the ditch!"—and then it righted itself and resumed.

"What the fuck you think you're doing, you trying to wreck us all?"

"Don't you what-the-fuck me. And leave her alone. You're getting to be just too goddamn mean for your own good."

Her precious beer haze was fading. Details sharpened: flesh and bone digging into her own, scratchy seat against her neck, the pain in her foot where it was twisted and jammed against somebody's boot. She was immobilized in the cramped space and the air was going bad. Under her buttocks she could feel the vibration of the tires that were catapulting them into darkness in their tin prison.

She hated this road. Highway 2 was all it was, really, running east through Smithville and a lot of little towns to the North Dakota border where she never had been; but there was a bad place on this stretch of the road, half-way between towns, where a lot of people had died. The railroad bridge over a long coulee was the landmark. "There? There?" she and Verna, little girls packed into the back seat of Alvin's car for the long trip to Lodgepole, used to cry. "Yeah, right there," Alvin would tell them without even looking to see where they were pointing. Gumma would click her teeth. She never would say a word about it. The Lodgepole cousins had told Verna and Junie the story Gumma never would tell. When they were older they, like Gumma, tried not to know it was there.

Junie wished she could look for the railroad bridge now, to be sure they was past the place, but the side windows were steamed over and she could not turn her head far. She hoped they were past it. Her legs ached where they were jammed between the seat and somebody else's legs, and she was afraid of what she smelled.

As a last resort she thought about Billy. Billy. He had been her true friend so long she had trouble remembering a time when she was without him. What she did remember was a blank space between Gumma and Billy when she could only look at her fingers, and Verna had screamed at her to wake up. How had she found Billy? She scowled and concentrated, but she could only remember the time with Billy and the time without him.

Her eyes widened as the car topped a hill and was filled with light that haloed the oval of Verna's stiff hair and froze for an endless split second the splash of beer that shot out of the can in Verna's hand as the driver wrenched the wheel around.

"Get over on your own side of the road!" the man beside Junie had time to bellow before the tires hit the gravel on the shoulder and shot sideways; they all were shouting, Verna's shrill "Aiiee!" cutting through it all; the driver still was fighting the wheel as they bucked over an embankment, the car seeming to take its own direction in angry single-mindedness. In the midst of pandemonium Junie's stomach was rolling back and forth like jelly and her head was snapping in countermotion, but she was wedged into the back seat too tightly to come loose. They still were in incredible motion, and she was sucking her own tongue, no Billy's cock the one thing she could do for him yes he liked it he lay back and looked at the ceiling while she sucked yes he never tried to put it in her nobody ever had except Alvin and after that Gumma ran him off Billy Billy Billy's cock and with a jolt that would have thrown her over the seat had she had space to move, they came to a halt.

A dead silence before the voices rose in recrimination.

"Christ he was coming right at me."

"You stupid goddamn son of a bitch you was driving on the wrong side of the road."

"Anybody hurt?"

"No but it wasn't because you knew what you was doing was it you loco goddamn—"

"Her? Naw she just bumped her head. Verna?"

"Ah-ah-bou—" Verna sputtered.

"See? There ain't no way of killing Verna."

"How the fuck we're gonna get out of this is what I want to know."

The man next to Junie opened the door and sprang out. Her grateful flesh expanded as cold air flowed over her. She could see the man walking around the front of the car in the headlights, bending over. "You're luckier'n hell," he shouted back.

"What happened?"

"You come up against a rock. Tore the bumper some is all."

"Try it in reverse."

Without waiting for the rear door to be shut, the driver

wrenched back on the gears and stepped on the gas. There was a lurch as the car freed itself and rolled backward over the grass with the rear door swinging wildly.

"Okay okay!"

Junie had gotten a whiff of gasoline. Her stomach, jolted and cramped and roiled, had had enough. It was roiling on its own. Junie's throat was hot. She panted for cold air, but it had come too late. She tried to move, at least lean away from the seat, but her stomach was contracting, had its spasm, and spewed its load.

Junie rolled her eyes toward the front seat, knowing she was in for it. The relief her stomach felt was almost enough to offset her apprehension. She hadn't been able to help it. From the puddle rose steam and a stench even in her own nostrils.

The man beside her was leaning to see—"What the hell?"

"Holy shit—" came the cry of outrage as the man in the black jacket came back around the car from his inspection of damage.

The driver leaned back. "She didn't—she did. In my car."

Junie began to cry.

"You sonsabitches, you had to drag her along."

"Get her the fuck out, maybe we can get rid of the worst of it—"

"No!" screamed Verna, scrambling to get out of the front seat and into the back. Somebody hauled her back down again. Junie could see her sticks of arms flailing over the back of the seat. She was being pushed toward the open door. She tried to say that she would get out by herself if they would give her time, but she lost her footing and rolled down the ditch. She saw the weeds and frozen gravel coming at her before she could get an arm up to absorb the brunt of the fall. Then she felt her face wrenched sideways and she hit the gravel and rolled, helpless as a turtle on its back, into the bottom of the borrow pit. Before the car door slammed she could hear Verna screaming something unintelligible, but she could not get her breath to answer.

She managed to raise herself enough to watch the car lumber around in the ditch. The headlights shone through the weeds and in her eyes, and for a moment she cowered for fear of what they would do, but then the car pulled back on the highway with a squeal of tires and shot off. Its taillights were lost over the next swell in the road.

For a time she lay on her back in the bottom of the borrow pit, a round dark hill of flesh, trying to get her breath. Even after her heartbeat steadied and she was able to breathe quietly, she lay still with her eyes closed, not uncomfortably, hearing the wind in the stubble fields and a bird's hunting call and a faraway motor. She opened her eyes and saw a clear sky and stars and the strobe lights of a tiny airplane, twinkling red pinpoints that cut a straight path across the stars.

At last the chill from the frozen sod found its way through the coat and made her uneasy. Her torn cheek had begun to tingle. Slowly she sat up, taking several tries at it and shifting her feet downhill before she could manage. She looked around and saw only weeds and the tops of fence posts against the night sky. No traffic. The back of her head throbbed, and there was a hurt in her side. One hand moved of its own accord to test the place, and she winced.

She had not thought about being afraid. She knew she could not be far from town, and if nobody came along to give her a lift, she always could walk. Remembering the carload that had left her behind, she knew she would walk. "Take her time," she told herself aloud, but the sound of a voice was so strange here in the weeds in the dark that she did not speak again.

With a grunt she got to her feet. Her head was oddly light, and she waited with her legs braced for the dizziness to pass before she began the climb out of the borrow pit. Taking a few steps at a time and resting in between steps, she at last tottered out on the shoulder of the road. Here she stood dead still while her head cleared, staring north across the asphalt and the railroad tracks to the clutch of shadowy cottonwoods in the bend of the river. The trestles of the railroad bridge stretched into the night.

She knew where she was. *It was wintertime and they all died. It was smallpox. They was camped by the river in the trees and you can still see their campfires if you go out there in the wintertime.*

You ever seen 'em?

Not me! I wouldn't go out there, but my uncle did and he said—

And as she stood now with her hands burrowing into her coat pockets for warmth and her feet on asphalt and the light night wind stinging the cuts on her face, the campfires began to appear. At first only a faint glow like a reflection on water, one by one they strengthed and flickered through the trees. She could see the bare winter branches silhouetted against the red firelight.

Even then she was not afraid. The play of flames beneath the bare trees was so warm that she even took a step into the road, thinking to cross it and roll under the barbed wire fence and find a path through the pasture to the camp where she could find a place by the fire. The campfires were a nest of lights mirrored a thousandfold in the night sky where the myriad twinkling bodies answered from their own paths. Stick and stone, flesh and blood, all one and all ringed by the lights.

She licked her lips. Almost, if she looked hard enough, she could catch sight of movement around the flames. The natural life of the camp unfolding as it ever had, season in and season out. Almost she could see the thickened body of a woman with a blanket over her head like Gumma's as she bent to put a stick on the fire—

—and my uncle, he was so scairt he said he wouldn't go back there for nothing in the world—

Gumma, she wanted to call out, but her lips were too stiff. Her heartbeat had hastened. She did stretch out a hand, but her vision blackened from the pain, for with the wind that chilled her mortal flesh came an awareness of the infinity that lay between the campfires and the dismal plateau where she had been abandoned to wait out her time

—and he says he can still see them lights right in his own head every time he thinks about 'em—

Her eyes were watering from the wind. Tears from the betrayal overflowed in hot trickles down her stiffened face. Even now from the stubble field behind her she could hear the whisper of paws and the faraway yip of a roaming dog or fox. Like an animal she was being doomed to watch the campfires from the shadows, like some shaggy feral thing that knew only blood or pain and nothing of the circle of the camp or the need to warm another's flesh. *Billy* had sustained her in the car as it plummeted; here it was only a word she dared not shape. In the face of this vision, no human love could sustain her.

The lights were brighter. At first with a wild hope she thought she had somehow been drawn nearer to the camp without knowing it; then she realized that one of the lights had detached itself and was moving at high speed down the road toward her. She knew what was happening, and she tried to prepare herself, although her heart was racing with fear. There were words for a woman to use in such a presence; her mind skittered back wildly to the deathbeds in the cabins and the words she dimly remembered the old women using, but of course they had been speaking in Cree. The very sounds she had been taught were alien. Since anything she could utter would be sacrilege, she allowed her hand to move before her breast in the sign of the cross she had been taught in school, knowing it belonged to the alleys and stenches she had left behind, but hoping it would be recognized as the only way she had of showing her awe.

The light was upon her, speaking in a mighty voice. *I know! I know!* flew her response as her arms opened wide to be received.

Alberta's Story

Sixty years is not a long time, and some of these old sandstone buildings have stood on Main Street ever since I can remember, but the Empire Cafe is the only business in town that is older than I am. As I pause with my hand on the door handle, I am looking straight into my own reflection in the dark glass and, wavering behind me like a bad memory all the more bitter for its lingering ghost of the familiar and well-loved, the outline of the gift shop and bookstore across the street where the old Bijoux Theater and Kale's Veterinary Supply used to be.

Any time I work up my nerve, I can open the door and step off the sunlit pavement onto soft pine flooring hollowed like a friendly palm. I can walk past the display case with its cigars and Life Savers under the rusty linoleum counter just as Father and I did every sale day and, unless Clay has beaten me to it, take one of the tables at the back where the faint rancid odor from the grill mingles and the smell of tobacco and spearmint to reassure me that something, at least, continues. And I might as well make up my mind to open the door as stand out here in the sun where Clay could come along any minute and leave me looking like a fool.

The iron door handle is smooth and warm as a familiar hand-clasp; more familiar than my own reflection which advances upon me, grinning lumpishly, and disappears as I pull open the door, on-ly to rematerialize out of the tarnished depths of the mirror behind the counter as I walk into the cafe. I avert my eyes too late not to see the dry frizz of hair under the Stetson and the sag of shirt and levis above and below my belt. Sixty years have settled without warning,and quite chapfallen is how I look.

But nobody is in the back except two men in white Dacron shirts drinking coffee and going over the figures jotted on a paper napkin. They hardly glance up as I take my usual seat with my back to the wall. Of course Clay wouldn't be here at this time of day, the sale won't be over for hours. *Unless the crew takes a coffee break. Unless for some reason he isn't working the sale this afternoon.* I catch myself hoping, and I cast around for a distraction. The menu, a typewritten sheet between limp gray plastic leaves, is wedged between the napkin dispenser and the salt and pepper shakers, and I think about ordering something to eat. A chicken-fried steak, perhaps. But it is too early in the afternoon to eat a heavy meal.

Debbie comes over to wipe the stains off the formica tabletop and set down a glass of water. "Are you having coffee, Alberta?"

"Please."

I must have been about nine years old the first time Father brought me in the Empire Cafe and ordered a chicken-fried steak. Had we been to a 4-H meeting? A bull sale?— There weren't many reasons why he would have taken me with him, which is why my memory of those times is so sharp. Mother, of course, never left the ranch, but that was on Margaret's account—at any rate, I wore a pair of brand-new levis, so stiff I could barely bend my knees, and I walked with dignity at Father's side. The cafe struck me with its grave air of men and their commerce, their unhurried comings and goings and pronouncements of the weather. It was town, what lay at the end of thirty miles of ruts leading in from the ranch, and it mattered. Sometimes even now I get a glimmer, a memory of a memory of how it felt to be driving into town, when I gear down the truck at the top of Main Street hill and look down at the familiar store fronts and cottonwood trees.

Debbie brings my coffee. "Are you going to order anything to eat, Alberta?"

"Oh—I don't know—" I think about consulting the menu, decide against it. "I guess just coffee."

Debbie slides her pad into her apron pocket and sits down to keep me company for a minute. "Wow, what a morning we had!" she sighs, lighting a cigarette. "It can stay slow all afternoon for all I care."

"I suppose all the boys came in from the yards for lunch today?"

I had asked it idly, and only when Debbie looks away do I realize how my question sounded to her.

"I guess they got a slew of consignments this morning. The boys were saying they'd be lucky to finish loading cattle and come in for supper by midnight," she says. From the way she keeps her eyes on the match she is putting out, I understand what she is telling me, and I ought to be grateful when I am only flooded with shame that Debbie, young Debbie, would *know*—

Everybody knows. —*at her age? Alberta got just what she was asking for. After all, he only married her to get his hands on the ranch. She must have known that. And you can't fault him for it. Not really. What could she have done with that ranch on her own? And she was no kind of a wife for him*—oh, I can hear them.

To shut out their echoes, I turn to Debbie. She is the only one of the Knutson girls to grow up with the looks and the calm of her grandmother. At one time I would never have believed it. Debbie, so bashful that her sisters had to drag her into her first 4-H meeting by force, squirming red and unable to answer the judge when he asked her about her yearling. It's hard for country children to get over their shyness, I ought to know—but Debbie, at least, had her sisters to play with, and she went to a real school when the time came. Debbie's grandmother and I—and Margaret, if she had been capable of learning to read—and a few others like Johnny Ware who grew up in the gumbo country before the roads were graveled had only the 4-H meetings and the correspondence courses we studied at home, which probably taught us more about books, at that, than schools do now. Shakespeare we read, and Sir Walter Scott. But there is so much more to learn.

Debbie has learned; she's done just fine. She has been saving her tips and wages from the Empire for three years so she can go away to the state university this fall.

"Have you done your clothes-shopping yet?" I ask her, and her face lights up as she talks of the sweater and slacks she has put on layaway and the down parka she would have bought—"but it was a hundred and fifty dollars, and I couldn't manage it and the dormitory deposit. All freshmen have to live in the dorm," she explains. Her hands gesture in humorous resignation—she is, after all, a girl who has rented her own room and looked after herself through four years of high school—and I notice how much older her hands look than the rest of her.

"You make me almost ready to go off to college myself," I joke. I mean to joke, at least, but she takes me seriously,

"Oh, Alberta!" Her young face is suffused with sympathy. "I never knew you wanted to go to college. And you never had the chance, always the work on the ranch coming first—"

"No, no! Really, Debbie. I meant to joke. All I ever wanted was the ranch."

But perhaps because she looks so doubtful, my words sound hollow to me even though I know they are true. For who would believe, after all, that the ranch was all I wanted? Clay didn't. *What's your story, Alberta?* he asked me the first week he was on the place. *How come you've hung around?*

"Just seems like it would be so lonely for you out there now." Debbie's eyes plead with me to take it in the spirit it is meant and not as meddling.

"Lonely? I wouldn't know what it means to be lonely," I scoff. Getting lonely wasn't a fashion in my day, or going off to college, either. Not that it necessarily is nowadays, from what I read. Debbie is behind the times, saving her tips for the state university because she is a country girl and she already has come so far—and I hate to think what she may find there—but then I remember the small weatherbeaten hands that are so at odds with the smooth brown hair and young face, and I reassure myself that Debbie will do just fine.

A shadow falls off the door, and I look up to see the angle of a stetson silhouetted against the bright sunlight and the line of shoulders that catches at my breath and draws the whole story so plainly across my face that Debbie has to avert her eyes.—*has she no shame, has she no pride? What did she expect, following, that she would find him doing in the granary? A man has a right to expect something better than a bag of bones like Alberta. The truth is, she as good as drove him to it. After all, what kind of a poor excuse for a woman is she?—has anybody ever seen her in a dress? and that house is a mess!—nobody's lifted a hand to clean it since her mother died—*

An instant is enough to set the rumors ringing in my ears and my face hot and cold and then drain me of all but a disappointment as sharp as a bad taste in my mouth as I see that the light has deceived me. It is not Clay coming past the counter, but only Johnny Ware, and of course I am not disappointed but relieved.

"Alberta," says Johnny, unsurprised, for of course he had the advantage of coming in with his back to the light and being able to see who was sitting in the back. Johnny hangs his hat on the back of a chair and eases his bones down, while Debbie runs off for a glass of water and the coffee pot.

Johnny watches her go. "She's the only one of those girls who's anything like her grandmother," he remarks.

"Debbie's getting prettier every day," I agree. But it isn't prettiness that makes me think of Lila. Fifty years ago when I started 4-H, Lila and Johnny were the big kids in the club, and we all depended on Lila even then. Now Lila is gone, and Johnny is so stove-up in the hips that for an instant I could mistake his walk for Clay's although Clay's broken bones come from the rodeo circuit and Johnny's from a lifetime of killing work on the ranch.

Debbie brings more coffee and goes off to clean up after the Dacron-shirt men, while Johnny settles down comfortably to drink his coffee and talk, as he can do for hours, of the weather and the roads and the grass this fall and the number of cattle trucked out of the country north of the river to be consigned at the stale this morning—"this is a big sale, but you won't see the big sales every week like they had six-eight years ago. Not that many cattle in this country any more. The boys all cut back on yearlings—price of feed what it is, they can't afford to raise cattle—" and while he talks, I think of all the sales Father and I worked together, earning money for the ranch, and the sales I worked with Clay after Father's accident.

I'd be working in the yards myself today, riding old Lightning up and down the center alley and hazing calves through the main gate into the sale barn, if it weren't for Clay. Avoiding Clay means staying away from the Wednesday sales, and driving past the Farmers Union without stopping for gas if his truck is parked by the pumps, and being afraid to walk into the Empire. That's the worst part.

No. The worst part is missing the sales, because of the money. Johnny is still talking, explaining something that Sim told him about the number of consignments they need every week to keep the cash flow at the yards high enough to pay overhead. He omits no details, and I can sip coffee and nod as though I am listening to more than every tenth word or so while my thoughts skitter off: *moneymoneymoney.*

Suddenly I wish I could tell Johnny about it. Through the dull flesh that has slipped from the bones of his face into bags and jowls, I can almost but not quite see *Johnny*, Johnny with the clean Ware features and blue eyes. How can I tell him anything? He's an old man, older than I am. What does he know? Years ago when we took the same correspondence course, Johnny and I made a game out of the verse quotations that headed every lesson. Oh, those lessons were full of knowledge about books. Even more than I, Johnny has grown up in a backwater. I am assuring myself that I cannot possibly tell him anything in the same instant that I hear my own voice blurt, "Johnny, I'm broke!"

Interrupted in the middle of a word, Johnny stares at me. His mouth has gone slack, but his face looks as if it could break into pieces, and I think unwillingly of Father's funeral and how Johnny began to cry at the graveside.

"It must get awful lonesome out there," says Johnny, getting the better of the wobble in his voice.

"Who said anything about lonesome? I'm never lonesome, I wouldn't know what it is to be lonesome! What I am is broke!"

Johnny nods. His old man's eyes, faded and inflamed, gaze on me but seem to see something else. "It's a damn fine ranch,"he says after a while.

"The ranch is all that counts with me. All the years Father put into it, and I—"

" Best pastureland in the country," says Johnny. "Too damn bad you can't make money running cattle any more."

"Johnny. As long as I could work at the stockyards, I could support the ranch. But—"

All at once I know I can't go on. Bad enough to make a fool of myself in public without having Johnny in tears. Debbie, arriving with the coffee pot, saves us both by pouring our cups full as if nothing in the world out of the ordinary were going on.

"After all Father and I did for him, took him in when he was too crippled up to work anywhere else—" *and then he took up with that bitch*—have I spoken aloud, when I meant to keep all complaints to myself? My fault, my own fault, I know.

Johnny sets his coffee cup down angrily. "No damn reason why you had to quit. Sim would sooner have you working for him than Clay."

"Yes, but Clay wouldn't have quit."

How can I explain that the world has divided into Clay's share and my share? His territory and mine, his friends and mine—and my share keeps shrinking as I let him take more. Like letting Margaret take what was on my plate because she didn't understand the difference—*the truth about Margaret, have you heard what Clay told? That she was really hers and old Albert's and that was why she was never right?—and her mother covered it up—*

Johnny looks as if he can read the rumors written right across my forehead. "You can't make a dime on it, but the land's worth a lot of money."

"I'd never sell it! It was Father's homestead, and now—"

"Still it can't be the same out there with everybody gone," says Johnny.

Against my will I remember how it used to be when the light in the kitchen meant Mother would be getting supper on the table and Margaret grinning out of her chair when Father and I came in from the chores. Margaret was good company. Mother never liked anybody outside the family to see her, but after her death, I used to take Margaret with me whenever I could, and she learned to recognize people and was glad to see them. But I couldn't sell the place. It would be like selling off Father. Johnny ought to know how it is, he's got a ranch of his own.

"Who gets it when you're gone?" Johnny wants to know. "There's only that nephew of your dad's left in the family."

"Junior? He'll get it eventually, I suppose."

Johnny snorts. "That damn fool. That jackass. I wouldn't want to see you do without a thing, Alberta, I wouldn't care what it was, just to see Junior turn around and sell the place after you're gone."

Johnny bangs his cup down loud enough to make a man buying cigarettes at the counter look our way. I don't know what to say. Of course I could sell. I know who'd buy me out in a minute and leave me the buildings and the horse pasture in the bargain.

"Hell, Alberta," says Johnny. "We all depend on you too much to have you giving up on us."

I have to laugh to myself. Coming from Johnny, of all people, when I always have known that a better woman would have handled things better.

A tiny memory surfaces, of going out to catch Lightning after a 4-H club meeting and finding Debbie sobbing behind the barn—

—Honey, what's wrong? To hear her, I would have thought somebody'd died. But no.

—I hate my mother! sobbed Debbie.

—Debbie, honey! People don't hate their mothers. I was thinking that Lila would have known what to say to her.

—I do. Debbie lifted a piteous face. I hate mine. I wanted to go with the boys, but my mother told me—tearful gulp—she told me I'm too big! She says no girl my age, no decent woman, hangs around the men and does men's work!

—Oh, Debbie—

I am jerked out of the reverie by the opening of the door to the street, and this time no glare of sunlight can blind me to his silhouette. Others are with him, the crew must have taken a break after all—but all I can focus on is that it wasn't disappointment I felt when it turned out to be Johnny walking into the Empire a little while ago, but relief. What I am feeling now leaves no doubt whatever. At least I don't have to worry about that.

"Of all the places in town the son of a bitch could go to drink coffee," somebody—is it Debbie?—hisses. I am half out of my chair, somehow getting the heel of my boot tangled in the absurd wire folderols on the chair leg, knowing I am red-faced and foolish.

Johnny's hand, horny-nailed and embedded with permanent grime, falls on my arm. "What have you got to run off for, Alberta? Sit down."

"But—"

"Sit down and let that son of a bitch walk out if he wants to!"

Johnny looks fed up with me, and I sink back in my chair, more taken aback by him than I am by Clay. The jigsaw fragments of my assumptions, blown apart by Johnny's anger, are filtering down like motes in the sunlight and beginning to reassemble in a new pattern that I could begin to perceive if I were not too frightened. *For of course I am guilty*—

Clay glances over his shoulder, laughs loudly, says something to the man next to him and nudges him. The other man's face turns blank, but my gorge is rising and I must run out or be sick—*keep my stinking carcass where he can't be disgusted*—

"You sit there and listen to me, Alberta. I've been hearing how he tracks you around town and runs you out of places, and it's all a lot of nonsense."

"Alberta," says Debbie, and it is toward her voice that I turn. "Don't you remember what you told me the time you found me crying?"

No, I don't remember telling her anything. What I remember is the stricken little girl and the dead certainty that what they accused me of was true. *Not a real woman, not Alberta. If she amounted to anything, she'd fold up and die like her mother. But not her, no, she stays healthy and goes to work right alongside the men. But she'll get what's coming to her. That rodeo hand, that's what's coming to her. Serves her right.* Is it possible that, for once in my life, instead of sinking willingly after the siren voices into the luxurious bog of self-hatred, I went right on saddling Lightning and said, *Work's work, Debbie! Been doing it all my life! Do you see me crying about what people say?*

Clay is standing there grinning, and the sloping line of his shoulders and the muscles of his neck are more familiar than the freckles and the loose skin I am always surprised to see on my own hands. Three weeks ago I could walk up to Clay and put my hand on his shoulder and feel warm. Now I have to watch that I don't reach out from force of habit, and the very air is divided between us: either his or mine to breathe.

Johnny hasn't budged. His back is turned to Clay, but his eyes don't spare me. Debbie is still standing behind me, so what can I do but sink back into my chair and pick up my coffee cup, which turns out to be empty? And lightning does not strike me dead, and thunder does not cleave the earth under me and let me fall through. All that happens is that Clay straddles a chair at the opposite table and starts to pick his teeth.

Johnny glares at me. "You just sit still a few times, and he'll quit."

The fragments have reassembled; the picture they form is painful, for all my hours of self-pity will buy nothing back, and nothing is going to happen except that Debbie will fill my empty cup. Still, clarity brings a certain relief.

And Johnny is right. It's not the same out at the ranch now. I think: I could keep the buildings and the horse pasture. Go back to work if I feel like it. And I can stop by Western Wear on the way out of town and have them lay back a down parka. She might as well look like the rest of those young kids that look like they're starting on a month's pack trip instead of on their way to class. Why not? I'm rich.

A Lesson
in Hunter Safety

Laura stood in the doorway of the VFW Club and peered into the dark sanctuary of middle-aged men. From along the bar and from tables farther back in the gloom the drowsy regulars roused themselves to stare at her, the intruder. The over-heated old cavern was thick with smoke and the smell of draught beer. Even the football game on the overhead television screen had been turned down so low that the flickering figures in uniform seemed like ghosts from a faraway world of combat come to haunt these sleepy and well-fed veterans.

The bartender hauled himself off his elbows and made his way down the bar toward Laura, squinting against the late afternoon sunshine that flooded through the door behind her.

"You bringing a kid to the hunter safety class? They're holding the meeting in the basement. Take the left-hand turn," he advised, and turned back to the game.

Apparently several parents and sons had been searching out the hunter safety course ahead of her and Robin. Self-conscious and pretending she did not see the row of sleepy eyes that opened wide enough to follow her, Laura sidled past the bar and went down the basement stairs. Robin, aloof but keeping so close that he was al-most trampling her heels, clutched the paper and pencil he had been instructed to bring.

She never had been in the VFW Club before. The odor of men going about their male doings made her edgy as a hunted thing even though she had seen them replete and satiated with beer. The lighted basement, with its sheetrocked walls and echoing cement floor, recalled less taboo suppers-and-bingo, but Laura still felt alien, and an old dread of opening a door upon a roomful of strangers kept her lingering at the foot of the stairs, examining a thirty-year-old tinted aerial photograph of VFW headquarters in

Pennsylvania that perhaps had been hung when the club was wide awake and active.

"Mother!" muttered Robin in her ear, and Laura opened the door.

Nothing had prepared her for the din. It still was only five minutes to seven, but the room was crowded with perhaps fifty squirming boys and a few girls. The racket made her think wildly of a giant chicken house at feeding time. She could not take her hand off the doorknob. Never had she encountered so much undirected energy. It boiled through the room, erupting in spurts of arguments or scuffles over the one or two remaining chairs. All the folding seats set out along the tables for the meeting had been taken by firstcomers who glared angrily at prowling invaders.

"I see now why they never advertise this class," said Laura over her shoulder to Robin.

Robin ignored her. Completing the hunter safety course was the only way he could get a license to hunt before he was sixteen, and he had made up his mind he was going to get a license.

"Over there," he said. Laura, following the jerk of his head, saw a row of filing cabinets across the back of the room. They offered a place to perch. Robin swung himself up and, after an involuntary glance over her shoulder to see if she were making herself conspicuous, Laura scrambled up beside him. Her legs dangled, exactly the same length as her son's, as like his as a twin in washed-out blue levis and cowboy boots.

But once she was high and dry in the corner, Laura felt at ease enough to watch the crowd. In the next ten minutes another twenty or thirty boys and a few fathers came down the basement stairs, looked with bewilderment through the door, and were sucked into the maelstrom. Boys were jostling two and three deep along the walls or hunkering down in corners.

The policeman who taught the hunter safety class, Fred Flisch, was dressed in an ordinary sports shirt and pants this evening, but he gripped a short rod like a swagger stick in front of him, and everyone knew who he was. His eyes, sunken above his chops, roamed over the racketing ten- and twelve- and fourteen-year-olds, counting them; and the boys sneered back at him, bright-eyed.

The three or four other adults in the room, men, were leaning back against the walls, resigned to the few minutes they had to spend in bedlam before they could leave and have a few beers until time to pick up their kids again. Meanwhile they shrugged and exchanged glances, glad it was Flisch and not themselves who had to face this pack of cubs. Mean little devils! Oh, everybody's kid was all right by himself, of course. Really decent. Maybe prone to a little trouble, like all kids. But a pack like this, all together? Flisch might be an ornery son of a bitch himself, but hell! Who else would tackle a job like this? And Flisch continued to pace the room, his back as broad and thick as a prime steer's, his eyes on the children.

Laura glanced at her son, wondering what he was thinking. Robin's face was unreadable under his heavy thatch of black hair. That was Robin, watching the world through skeptical dark eyes that never missed a thing and never gave a thing away. When he was a toddler strangers had stopped to look at the striking little boy with the beautiful dark eyes. Now at thirteen he was slim and dark and shaggy and had the beginnings of a moustache on his upper lip. He was growing almost visibly. In a few months Laura wouldn't be able to borrow a pair of clean levis from him the way she had this evening. But the surge of good feeling came back to remind her: *at least she had done a good job with Robin.*

She felt someone watching her from across the room and looked up to see Flisch's assistant, a beefy young man with a crew cut and jowls like Flisch's who wore a fluorescent orange hunting vest as buoyant as a life jacket. Laura had noticed him earlier, pretending to be counting stacks of hunter-safety booklets but all the time stealing looks at the pandemonium behind him, and she had recognized his fidgeting as teachers' stage fright. Laura now dropped her eyes, blocking off the familiar inward taunts that rang louder than all the racket of the hunter safety class. *Does he know who you are? Something about you? Or is it just that not many women come to this class? It's probably supposed to be for fathers and sons.*

Boys kept pushing into the room, jostling others and raising tides of protest. Laura thought there must be a hundred of them. The air had gone stuffy.

At last Flisch stopped his pacing. His knuckles glistened on his short rod. "How many you kids under twelve?" he demanded.

About half the pack raised their hands. Everybody looked around to see if their friends were raising their hands, took their own hands down, argued with their neighbors over how old they were, changed their minds.

"All you guys under twelve, you're gonna have to leave. We're gonna run another class in a few weeks. You can take hunter safety then."

"Awww!" rose the wail. They wanted to take the class right now. Right now!

"If you're under twelve, you can't go hunting this year anyway. You have to be at least twelve before it's legal. You can come back in a few weeks. We'll have another class organized."

At last about thirty of the younger boys were chased out, complaining as they went. Even then there were not enough application forms to go around, and Flisch's assistant went to bring another stack.

Robin was passed an application card and an instruction manual. Laura got an orange NRA booklet entitled "When Your Boy or Girl Asks for a Gun." The sketch of the smiling American family on the cover reminded her of a picture from a child's primer. Robin scowled at the booklet from under his dark shag of hair.

"They ought to have a picture of the old man in his undershirt, yelling how he'll break the kid's rifle over his head if he don't leave him alone," Robin hissed.

"You'd better be quiet," said Laura. But to herself she was pleased. Robin never had bogged down in the slough of the predictable where so many of her students seemed permanently mired. He never would be sucked into a pack. At least she had taught him to question, to consider. The implied criticism of his father she probably ought not to allow; her twinge of guilty pleasure told her so. But it was Robin's own assessment. At least he thought for himself.

Flisch's assistant, sounding angry as he raised his voice to be heard, explained how the application card must be filled out, where the parent or guardian must sign, and how the kids could get their hunting licenses at half price if they asked for student tags and showed their hunter safety cards. Robin had filled out his card before the assistant could finish his explanation. He handed it to Laura to sign.

"Where'd you say to put our names?" shouted a very small boy in the back of the room. His cry loosed a torrent.

"We supposed to turn these in now?"

"What'd you say?"

"What'd you say?"

"Hold it down!" Flisch bellowed. He patrolled the room, stepping over legs and gripping his little rod, while his assistant explained everything all over again. Laura turned the application card over and looked at the blanks Robin had filled with his cramped penmanship.

"Do you really want to do this?" she asked. At first she had thought he was joking when he had announced that he was going to attend the hunter safety class and get his hunting license. She still could not be certain he was serious. Looking at him now, she was struck as she had been a thousand times at how much Robin was like her. The velvety fringed eyes and the soft dark skin, even the rounded limbs exactly the same size as hers under the denim shirt and the blue levis washed to velvet. A part of her, exactly like her except for the silken moustache beginning to claim his upper lip like insidious, growing maleness.

"Mother!" said Robin, annoyed. "We already talked about that. And Granddad's counting on it." He reached over and repossessed the card she already had signed.

Now Flisch was explaining the requirements for passing the hunter safety course while the assistant took a turn at prowling up and down, bumping into legs and elbows, and glaring down impudent grins. His resentful gaze strayed to Laura on her file-cabinet perch, and she willed herself still.

All the children had to pass the hunter safety course before they could get a hunting license. That much Flisch could hold over them. Otherwise no legal hunting, no rifle until they were sixteen.

He read aloud a list of rules called the Ten Commandments of Hunting.

"You will know these by heart," he said, glaring around at the smirking boys who had crawled around behind him. "Word for word. We're gonna give you a test, and you have to get 88 on it to pass. The national requirement, it's only 80, but here in Hill County we say you have to have 88."

One boy raised his hand. "What if we don't?" And his friends tittered, as delighted as if he had posed an unanswerable dilemma.

"Then you don't get no hunting license. And furthermore. It don't matter what you get on that test. Even if you get 100 percent on that written test, it still don't matter. We got to sign it where it says you passed. And we catch one of you pulling *some stunt*—" he paused to let the words sink in, walking the length of the room with his stick gripped hard in front of his belly while the boys behind him caught each others' eyes and quivered with the held-in giggles—"we catch you pulling *some stunt*, you're never gonna get no license. We'll pull your card and that'll be the end of it, no matter what you get on that written test. No way you'll get to hunt till you're sixteen."

The boys began to snicker. Scuffles broke out all over the room, intensified by the heat and the crowd of young bodies intruding against others. They punched each other, pretending they were being funny about it, but the glitter of their eyes gave them away. Application cards were snatched, torn, spun from hand to hand. Noise rose like a tidal wave and Laura, crouching back on the file cabinet, remembered the men in the bar upstairs, entrenched over their beer and lulled by the silent combat of the televised football game. It was a wonder the ceiling didn't buckle under them.

"All right, all right! Let's keep it down!" shouted Flisch. He and his assistant stalked up and down the room, their faces pulled into masks threatening a grim fate to whelps who failed to take hunter safety seriously. The weight of their faces dragged order among the children nearest them, but chaos and laughter broke out as soon as the adults moved on. But there was a change; their inward antagonism had turned into united defiance of the adults.

"That prick Flisch is gonna get his!" hissed Robin. Laura, glancing up, saw that her son's eyes gleamed out of a face as flushed as the other children's.

"Robin!" she said, appalled.

"Well, you know what he did to Mike Worrick's brother! I suppose you think that's hot stuff! I suppose you think a kid *deserves* to have his ribs broken—"

"I didn't say anything of the kind!" began Laura in an angry whisper, but Robin already had withdrawn from the argument. He was listening intently to Flisch, who somehow had been drawn off on a patriotic tangent.

"We live in a great state. The greatest. You want to appreciate Montana, you go someplace else to live for awhile and try to go hunting or fishing there. You're gonna run into garbage everywhere, and you're gonna meet people who got no respect for nobody or nothing. You gotta go see it to believe it."

Robin was expressionless, but his eyes slid around to see how Laura would respond.

"What's the matter?" she whispered, knowing it was a test.

"Nothing." He withdrew again, offended. Laura could feel from the stiff flesh of his young neck and arms that he was pained at her refusal to share his disgust. And yet she sensed still another barrier. Would Robin *let* her agree with him? From across the room Flisch's assistant, almost submerged by the turbulence of the pack in spite of his billowing orange jacket, also was watching her. Laura kept her own face carefully blank.

The current story about Fred Flisch going around the college campus had to do with a house party he had raided a few weeks ago. The kids had had no warning and couldn't get rid of whatever it was, mescaline or something—or worse yet, according to the preferred version among Laura's students, they would have had plenty of time to flush whatever it was down the toilet except that Flisch had bulled his way inside and worked over a couple of the boys. The students said that one of the boys had had a cracked rib, another a ruptured spleen. Laura hadn't believed them. Not that

Flisch was incapable of it; she could believe almost anything of those slow furious eyes and the meaty hands locked on their stick. But surely no parent would remain silent?

Or would they? For the basement tonight seethed with the hostility of sixty or more boys who, after a few meetings like this one, were to be armed with rifles and loosed on the countryside for hunting season with cards stating that the possessor knew the Ten Commandments of Hunting and had passed the test with a score of 88. Laura found herself hoping they all had responsible fathers before she realized that she, Flisch, and Flisch's assistant were the only adults in the room. The others had dropped off their children and made their escapes. For some reason the father-son sketch on the cover of the hunter safety booklet must have caught her imagination.

"After all," Flisch was telling the boys, "we've been around for awhile. We've seen a thing or two. We're just telling you, same as your dads would. And we ain't perfect, I wouldn't try to tell you that. Like, we don't always bring in the game. We get skunked, same as your dads do sometimes. No," Flisch conceded, "we're not perfect."

"Don't you listen to him," the assistant spoke up. His mouth smiled while his eyes roved anxiously back and forth above the ricture, seeking rapport with the pack at any cost. "Him—" the spaniel eyes turned to Flisch—"him, he got a nice six-point elk last year. Me, I was the one got skunked." His laugh, divided between Flisch and the pack, begged them all to be guys together, one good bunch of people.

"Wonder if I should tell him what my dad got!" sneered Robin.

"Robin!" said Laura, for once more disturbed than pleased at his jab at his father. The tide below her was swelling, and it seemed to her that not even Flisch could keep a semblance of order much longer.

Oblivious, however, Flisch had begun a lecture on how they should clean up after themselves. "It makes me sick to find garbage everywhere, even way out in the hills. Probably dumped by one of them that don't have no respect for this country or themselves either. I catch any of you throwing beer cans or *whathaveyou—*"

the long rhetorical pause, the glare around the room—"or *whathave you*, I'll skin you myself."

Flisch's assistant began to tell a story.

"Some of you may know Steve Lambert, he runs the western goods store here in town. Well, his father, old Saylor Lambert, he's got a ranch down by Cascade. South of here."

Laura's attention was distracted from Robin. She too had lived south of Cascade, and she remembered Saylor as an old man who kept a tight thumb on all he owned.

"Old Saylor Lambert, he's got a fishing pond on that ranch of his. We went down here, me and Mr. Flisch—" the spaniel eyes made the acknowledgement—"and we fished his pond. We didn't have no luck. And beings I wasn't getting no bites, I figures I may as well do something. So I gets one of them net onion sacks like I always carry in the camper. I starts gathering up beer cans, all kinds of crap, from around that pond.

"Pretty soon here comes old man Lambert in his pickup. 'I been watching you through my field glasses from the top of that hill,' he says. 'You seen the guys that threw all this crap around my pond?'

"'No,' I says, 'I ain't seen nobody. But I've been gathering up this garbage for an hour.'

"'I know you have,' he says to me, 'I've been watching you. And I want you to know, any time you want to hunt or fish on my land, that's fine. You're always welcome. But that son of a bitch that left those beer cans here, I'm gonna shoot that son of a bitch if I ever catch him. And I'm layin' for him on the top of that hill.'"

Boys were yelling all over the room. Laura could not hear the end of the story, or the moral if it had a moral.

"Sick!" sneered Robin, and she turned to him, but just then a scuffle broke out in the corner behind the file cabinets. A boy, shoved by a companion, lurched into Laura and recovered himself without ever being aware of the contact. He threw himself at the boy who had shoved him. Robin launched himself silently at the invader's retreating back.

"Robin!" she cried.

"Hold it down!" bellowed Flisch. "We're just about out of time tonight anyway!"

Somehow his voice just overrode the tide. He soldiered on, giving instructions about the next class meeting and what the boys should bring with them, promising pictures of hunting accidents. "We'll let you see just what it looks like to have half of your head blown off because you used the wrong gauge shell in your shotgun."

By now every boy in the basement was howling at his neighbor, but the effect was for Flisch. Their eyes were fixed on Flisch, their mouths frozen in grins as they waited for him to make his move. Robin leaned against the file cabinets, his young shoulders quivering and his eyes shining. Even on her high perch Laura was jostled again; then Robin was shoved back against her, pinning her leg at a painful angle between his shoulder blades and the cabinets. He lunged away, pummeling the other boy.

Flisch's assistant had retreated to the row of locked gun cabinets at the rear of the basement. His widened, fearful eyes found Laura's again, and Laura abruptly drew her knees up against her chest and hugged herself on her small threatened island. The other adults had been wise to depart, she realized. Afraid of their own children and yet reluctant to brutalize them into obedience. They'd rather Flisch did it for them.

"Same time tomorrow night!" shouted Flisch. "Don't forget to learn your Ten Commandments!"

At last he yielded to volume, stepped aside, and let the pack storm the stairs.

Laura waited on her high-and-dry cabinet until the basement was cleared of all but the stragglers who already had lost their application cards or who had had them snatched away. Robin surfaced from a hooting tangle of arms and legs and went up to Flisch to turn in his card.

Laura slid off the cabinet and waited for him. Maybe she should not have signed his card. But she knew she couldn't have denied him. She would have been acting like a nervous mother hovering over the boy growing up without a father. It was her fault he didn't have a father; the least she could do was see he grew up normally.

Flisch took Robin's card. His eyes, weary in his overfed face, flicked over Laura and registered nothing. He seemed deflated in the nearly empty room. The electric light fell straight down from the ceiling; he did not even cast a shadow.

After all, nothing had happened.

"Mother!" said Robin. His face was flushed. "Can I go with Mike?"

"Mike who?"

"Mike Worrick."

"I thought you and I were going out for pizza afterward."

"Yes, but—Mother! These guys are going to the Dairy Queen. And I can walk home with Mike!"

They were halfway up the basement stairs. Robin was a step ahead of her. Laura had to look up to meet his hot, urgent eyes. "I don't know," she said. She had looked forward to the evening with Robin. She remembered how she had worried whether he would make friends his own age here.

Someone was climbing the stairs behind them. Laura hastily made way for Flisch's assistant. "Excuse me!"

"That's okay," said the young man. His arms were full of hunter safety pamphlets. Lugging the pamphlets, he followed Laura and Robin out of the basement.

"Mother!" Robin urged.

"Oh. Go ahead. Watch out for the traffic on College Avenue. It's getting dark."

"Can I have a dollar for a hamburger?"

Laura dug in her handbag and found a dollar bill. The younger Worrick boy, she saw, was waiting in the doorway of the VFW Club. A few other boys lingered on the street corner, expecting a ride or perhaps killing time on their own.

"Some class, right?"

It was the young man, Flisch's assistant.

"I wouldn't want to try to teach it," Laura agreed. Robin had snatched his dollar and run off with Mike.

"Yeah—" he leaned against the wall with his armload of pamphlets, trying to make conversation. "A lot of folks think Fred, he's too rough on them kids. But you saw what it was like."

131

"Yes."

"And it's worse, other places. You know there's schools where they got policemen right there in the halls?"

"Yes," said Laura.

"Hell, some adult's gotta be in charge. Only thing is, when it's you and you know you got no answers, it makes you wonder. Right?"

He risked a laugh.

"Yes," said Laura for the third time. Unwillingly she recalled the panic of her first year of college teaching. The awkward young man waited, trying to think of something else to say. Laura retained an image of him armed with a nylon net sack that once had contained onions, attacking the edge of an avalanche of debris.

"You wouldn't care to stay and have a beer?" he asked.

"No," she said politely. "I have to get home."

It was almost dark. The streetlights made a cavern of light across the town, but the September wind was sharp against the corners of buildings and the parked cars. Children still roamed the street. A parting jeer floated back through the evening gloom. Somewhere ahead was Robin. Laura shivered as she left the dusty shelter of the VFW Club and made her way into the chill.

Kissing
My Elbow

When I was thirteen I discovered that time, mysteriously, was something other people tried to catch and hold. Aunt Rhoda talked of little else. "I don't know how many of them will expect to stay for supper," she said that summer, frowning up at her old adversary the kitchen clock. "The cold chicken and ham will go around, but there's the bread to slice and the pies to warm up, so expect to be back here by four o'clock, girls, and plan for five o'clock. It all takes time, and you can't let men sit and wait for a meal. You might as well understand that, first as last!"

"First as last! First as last!" complained Eleanor as soon as we were out of earshot of the kitchen. "That's all I've heard all summer, Juley."

The wet velvet lawn and the wrought iron fence that kept the livestock out of Aunt Rhoda's lilacs seem as improbable to me now as an illustration out of a magazine. Nothing of Aunt Rhoda's resembled the ordinary farm yards and vegetable patches of the kin she'd married among. Even her tomato plants were disciplined on stakes. The orderliness made the eroded river bluffs and ploughed benchland seem out of place and not the other way round. I liked it better in the fierce sunlight once Eleanor and I reached the road, and yet Aunt Rhoda's order excited me; I think even then I wondered if I were running to it or from it.

My cousin Eleanor never had doubts. That afternoon she stopped dead in the road at the first whiff from the shearing sheds and argued against going to watch. "Wait!" she yelled when I started ahead alone. "You can't hear yourself think down there. Let's go back to the house. I want to show you something."

"I want to watch them shear," I yelled back.

Sheep-shearing was the din of a thousand ewes and lambs drowning out the sound of the river running past the pens and the shouts of the men and even Eleanor's voice. My wanting to do the opposite of what she told me sent me climbing up the board fence to lean against a post in the sun and watch the milling sea of gray fleeces below me. I could see my father with his back turned, and my big cousins, Hoot and Jake, that I wanted to grow up to be like, and the crew of Hutterites Uncle Joe had hired to shear. The Hutterites were the fastest shearers in the country, but hard on the sheep. At dinner my father had said one of the ewes was going to die from her cuts, but Uncle Joe never even looked up from his place.

"Come on, Juley," whined Eleanor, but I settled myself against the post with the sun burning down on my hair and watched Darius Stahm shear a sheep.

He had a system. He and his bearded brothers Eli and Paul had run their extension cords and set up their electric shearing rigs at ten-foot intervals across the pen, and there they labored with their blades, three executioners in black, while their black-garbed sons wrestled the unsheared and struggling ewes right up to the rigs and then (the job I had expected to do before I got shanghaied into the kitchen) hazed off the clipped and dazed victims. Unlike the other neighbors, who would take time to laugh about the work and drink beer, the Hutterites never wasted a minute. They were like a tribe of ants, each going about his business with never a request for help. They even had brought along one of their girls to serve their noon meal on the grass above the pens. "Didn't they think my food was fit to eat?" asked Aunt Rhoda. Then she said she guessed she should be glad they didn't expect to be served in her kitchen.

Below me in the corral, Darius Stahm took a struggling ewe from one of the black-clad boys and sat her on her tail between his knees. The ewe stopped kicking; her eyes glazed as Darius brought his electric blades up her belly to peel back the gnarled gray fleece. The way she submitted to the clippers, her tongue protruding and all four feet sticking out from between Darius' broad thighs, made me a little sick.

Darius finished shearing the ewe and let her go. She took an unsteady step or two in her new naked state before the boys chased her off. Darius took time to straighten his back before he took the next sheep, and when he looked up, he caught me watching him. In turn, I was caught by a good-humored face full of whiskers and spectacles and a broad gold smile. He called out something I couldn't hear and motioned to me. Embarrassed, I tried to look away, but he kept smiling and waving the blades at the sheep. It seemed a mile from my perch to the ground, but I slid down, and I remember how insignificant I felt beside big Darius in his green gingham shirt and suspenders and home-sewn black trousers as he put me between himself and the sheep and showed me how to hold the blades—and why did I climb down from the post and try, if not because I felt myself slighted that morning, made to do girls' work?

As he showed me how to hug up against the woolly back, I began to relax and pay attention to what he was demonstrating. His arms felt like my father's, and his big hands, work-grimed and cracked around the nails like my father's, were reassuringly deft with the blades. The next moment the blades were in my hand, moving with what felt like their own accord to peel back the fleece. The ewe lay in frozen astonishment between my legs as the gray hide and pink creases emerged from her own wool. Darius' hand was there to guide the blades around the difficult juncture of legs and body, and then I was shearing by myself again. I left a ragged ridge of wool behind the blades, bit deeper, and saw a spreading rivulet of bright red blood against the gray.

"Iss okay!" Darius roared in my ear. I sheared grimly, trying to keep the blades steady and not cut the ewe again. I was making an uneven job of the fleece, but I could see that with practice I could shear as well as anybody.

The weight of the fleece, thick and gray and rank with lanolin, fell back over my thighs as it peeled away. I never had felt anything so heavy. And gradually the ewe emerged, stupid and stark, with her pink udder and the creases around her hindquarters exposed behind the heavy wool. My ears were full of the electric motor, my throat clogged with dust. Then the last ragged ends of wool fell away from my lap, and the ewe rolled over and stood up. One of the boys yelled and stamped at her until she tottered away to the outer pen where her lamb, newly vaccinated and jerking a bloody stump where they had docked his tail, was bleating for her.

The other boy was wrestling up a fresh ewe, but Darius took charge of this one. I stepped back against the fence. I had sheared my sheep. My arm was numb from the vibration of the shears, and my legs, freed from the weight of the fleece, felt as unstable and empty as balloons.

Eleanor poked me through the fence, mouthing something. "What?" I asked. But I had to climb the fence and slide down on the other side before I could hear her hiss: "How do you think it looks for you to practically sit on one of their laps?"

Uncle Joe came trotting around the end of the pen. "That girl of Darius'!" he shouted at Eleanor. "She's sick. Touch of the sun. You take her up to the house and get her a drink of water and let her sit somewhere cool."

The girl was a shadow through the glass of Darius' truck. She had been sitting there and knitting all day in the long hot clothes her religion made her wear. The men hadn't even bothered to park the truck where she could be in the shade.

We passed my father, cleaning vaccine guns and sorting out the unused ampules by the east fence. "Dad," I said, "Darius showed me how to shear a sheep."

"I saw you."

The tone of his voice was so shriveling that I could not move. I started to defend myself, but he looked up from his vaccine guns and impaled me with his furious blue eyes. "It's one thing if you have to show off around home. But it looks like you could act your age when the rest of the neighborhood can watch you."

To say his anger was incomprehensible to me was to say the least. He had always been proud of me, called me his boy—what had I done to deserve this?

In retrospect, it seems to me that his anger was the beginning of the dissolution that has left me where I am today: safe, in a way, with the marriage behind me; high and dry, certainly; happier now that my position at the hospital is primarily administrative. At the time, I only knew I never had felt such a wrench. Can a girl experience the breaking of an umbilical cord between her and her father?

By then Darius had come along, and they had the Hutterite girl out of the truck. "You just go along with Eleanor!" Uncle Joe told her loudly, but she stood yellow-faced and meek until Darius spoke to her in German. Then she shuffled off after Eleanor, keeping an arm's length behind her.

I tagged miserably along to watch. Besides the dark scarf tied over her twisted hair, the Hutterite girl wore a shapeless dark blue bodice and an ankle-length greenish skirt with a green apron over it. On her feet were boys' shoes. Between the shoes and her hem were her naked ankles, white and sparsely haired. As we climbed the trail to the road and cut across Aunt Rhoda's sheer lawn into the shade of the elms, I caught a whiff of the girl's faint foreign body odor. It made my hackles rise.

Eleanor led us past the honeysuckle and into the empty kitchen. She pulled a chair out from the table, and after a moment's hesitation the Hutterite girl sat down on the ruffled cushion. Her back was rigid. She accepted the glass of water Eleanor handed her and took one small sip.

"What's your name?" asked Eleanor loudly, but the Hutterite girl only hunched her shoulders under her ill-fitting bodice. "She probably can't speak any English," said Eleanor.

"I thought they learned in school," I mumbled.

"Eleanor!" called Aunt Rhoda from the bedroom, and Eleanor groaned and went to see what she wanted. The Hutterite girl's eyes, as if freed by Eleanor's departure, took a fugitive tour of the kitchen with its blooming geraniums and red-checked ruffles that looked like a picture in a magazine. Looking at her hunched mute figure spurred my anger. What did she have to feel miserable about?

Eleanor flounced back. "She just wanted to know what was going on. She isn't too happy about *her*. Or you, either." Eleanor giggled. "She says your mother ought to know better than to let you turn tomboy."

All I could hear were ordinary sounds, the hum of Aunt Rhoda's electric clock and the faint rattle of the refrigerator clicking on, and behind it somewhere the faraway sound of the expensive pump that brought water into Aunt Rhoda's kitchen.

"Actually," Eleanor was saying, "she isn't that bad looking."

"I think she looks awful."

The Hutterite girl's nose twitched. It was a thick, white nose with red veins at the nostrils. A sheep's nose.

"Not if she had decent-looking clothes," said Eleanor. "What do you think she'd look like in nice clothes?"

"I don't know," I said. "Like anybody." And I stood up.

"What are you going to do?" said Eleanor. "No. Listen. We shouldn't make her do something her father wouldn't like." But her face was alive with curiosity. "Do you think she'd look like us?"

I took the Hutterite girl by the elbow and, when I felt her flesh shrink away, shoved her toward the door. The sight of her scared blue eyes, set wide apart over raw, foreign cheekbones, made me contemptuous. I was pretty certain by then that my father was angry because I practically had sat in a foreigner's lap. The Hutterite girl might as well have gotten me in trouble herself.

Eleanor had been using the glassed-in back porch for a bedroom that summer. Aunt Rhoda had cleared out the litter of stacked egg cartons and fruit jars and feed sacks, hung curtains all the way around, and set up a cot for her. Eleanor had added a pink chenille bedspread from home and set a doll with a wide pink and white skirt made from milk strainers on the old oak bureau under the mirror.

"This is what I wanted to show you," said Eleanor. She took a pink angora sweater from behind the curtain where she hung her clothes.

An aureole of fibers followed my finger and caught on my rough skin when I reached out to touch it. The wool was incredibly soft.

Eleanor smiled. "It was the first thing I bought with my money. Made it almost worth waiting on her all summer." But she laid the sweater on the bed. "Here's something she can try on."

She took down a pink cotton dress with a white collar and held it in front of the Hutterite girl, who winced back as if it were hot.

"After I fix her up," said Eleanor, taking charge, "I'll start on you, Juley. You need fixing up as much as she does."

"I do not."

"You wait till high school starts and see how you feel then."

Eleanor laughed. "Listen, do you know why Darius offered to teach you to shear that sheep? He thought you were a boy!"

"He didn't either," I said. "How do you know?"

"I heard him tell Uncle Joe." Eleanor laughed again. "I guess he felt pretty funny when he caught on."

I remember how, through a hot glaze of blood, I looked into Eleanor's watery mirror and saw my own reflection. My hair was as short as any of the Hutterite boys', my breasts (as they are today) hardly more than plump nipples, completely obscured by the baggy folds of the shirt of my father's I had worn that day because I had expected to be helping in the pens. But *no*! Surely Darius had offered the blades to *me*!

"Let's see what she looks like under this scarf," said Eleanor.

Understanding too late what Eleanor intended, the Hutterite girl gave only one squeak as the scarf came off and, its knot still tied, fell on the bed. I stared in spite of my own misery, because I never had seen a Hutterite woman's hair. This girl's hair was pale brown and so thin that her scalp showed white where the hair was pulled harshly back into a twist. Fine escaping hairs had followed the scarf and stood on end like a frightened halo. All I could wonder was how she could stand to be so ugly.

Eleanor was undoing the long row of hooks and eyes. The Hutterite girl made a half-hearted attempt to snatch back her clothes, then crossed her arms to hide her chest. I saw that she wore no brassiere nor even an undershirt, though her breasts were very heavy. Against all that white flesh, the girl's sunburned hands seemed to belong to someone else.

"Hand me the dress," said Eleanor.

But now she met resistance. Without actually battling, the Hutterite girl seemed determined not to let the pink cotton descend over her head. Every time Eleanor advanced with the billowy folds, she managed to duck and squirm away. She wedged her chin against her collarbone and drew her shoulders up tight against her neck. At last she even took her hands away from her breasts to push away the dress.

"Juley, help me!" Eleanor snapped. She was damp with effort.

I got off the bed where I had sat down to watch. I didn't want to touch the other girl again. I could smell Eleanor's wet skin and the odd foreign odor of the Hutterite girl. I wiped my hands against my blue jeans and saw that a strand of pink angora still was sticking to a callus. For some reason it reminded me of my own misery, and I strode up and grasped the Hutterite girl by the wrists and drew her hands down so Eleanor could lower the pink dress over her head.

But the Hutterite girl still resisted, ducking her head lower and lower until she was crouched in a ball at our feet with her limp greenish skirts falling around her.

"Let's leave her alone," I said. I had things to think about. The brooding afternoon teased at me and drew my mind away, and indeed I might have slunk away by myself and wallowed in my predicament until I was ready to grovel for my father's forgiveness, had not the Hutterite girl at that moment turned on me, bared her tiny gray teeth, and sank them into my arm.

I gasped and jerked away. The bite had not been hard; the circle of toothmarks was less distinct than the wet ring of saliva, but I suddenly was consumed with rage. I scoured my arm against my blue jeans before the girl's spittle made me retch, and then I snatched the pink dress out of Eleanor's hands and advanced upon the foreigner.

Taken by surprise, the Hutterite girl's resistance fell briefly away. Over her head went the dress, its folds falling to her knees. With wrath and joy I groped for her arm and jerked it through a sleeve.

But by now she was fighting back, as sturdy as any of my cousins. Together we squealed and fought and lunged against the oak bureau, wildly rocking Eleanor's collection of earrings and trinkets before I got the other arm through a sleeve. The Hutterite girl fell back, gasping, clad in torn pink. She and I stared at each other in dawning recognition.

"Oh God, the men are back!" cried Eleanor, running to the window.

I dropped my arm and unclenched my fist. I would only have been hitting myself.

As my eyes cleared, I saw that the Hutterite girl was struggling with the unfamiliar fastenings of Eleanor's dress. I stared at her flushed face, taken aback by her genuine fear.

"They're here!" hissed Eleanor.

I helped the Hutterite girl get Eleanor's pink dress off her neck. Clumsy with haste, we found her rumpled blue bodice and her scarf. We could hear the men at the gate, talking on the way up the walk, as I feverishly hooked the dozen fasteners up the back while the other girl crammed her hair back under her kerchief. We nearly fell over each other in the rush to get through the door and down the hall to the kitchen.

Uncle Joe just was opening the kitchen door. "Feeling better?" he inquired cheerfully.

"Yes," said Eleanor.

I stole a look at the other girl. She looked flushed but collected as she sidled over to Darius and stood by him. Uncle Joe was getting his checkbook down from the top of the refrigerator while Jake, who didn't give a damn if he was in Rhoda's kitchen, helped himself to beer. All the men were crowding in and opening bottles of beer, jostling and dirty and glad the shearing was done. All but Darius, of course; Hutterites only drank the unsweetened wine they made themselves, and they didn't know what it was to be neighborly.

He accepted his check from Uncle Joe. I thought he looked like a big bearded black bear in the midst of my rowdy cousins. I couldn't bring together the good-natured gold-toothed smile that had encouraged me down from the fence with the fear in the other girl's eyes. But I knew her fear had been real.

"Sure, sure," Darius was saying to Uncle Joe's repeated invitation to come and shear again next year. Then he nodded to his girl and took himself out of Aunt Rhoda's kitchen. She followed without a word. I caught just a glimpse of her expressionless face under her spotted kerchief.

Aunt Rhoda came out of her bedroom. "Are they gone?" she asked. "I didn't like to come out until I knew they were gone." She looked around at Joe's cousins and brothers, crowding her pretty kitchen with their grimed faces and their bottles of beer. Her nostrils widened at the common stench.

"Best help I ever had," said Joe, "and I hope I can get them next year."

Everybody else bristled. Jake's eye, searching for an objection, lit on me. I knew I was in for it. "Good help, all right!" Jake shouted. "Old Darius, he helped Juley right into his lap! Did you like that, Juley? Did you like shearing sheep?"

They all were looking at me. "She prob'ly did," said Hoot. "Remember when she used to try to kiss her elbow because somebody told her it would turn her into a boy?"

My father's eyes were chips of blue in his blackened face as he waited to hear what I would say. I knew I could join in Jake's ridicule and wear it as a cloak if I wanted to. But I didn't want to. It wasn't a question of choosing between us and the foreigners, as I would have thought an hour ago. It was choosing me, no matter where that left me, and I think even then I sensed it might leave me high and dry. If you're not a boy and won't be a girl, what are you? Me, that's who, although for years, and especially since time, for me as it once was for others, has changed to something to catch and hold, I have wished and half-believed there was another alternative.

Aunt Rhoda thought the cat had my tongue. "You boys leave Juley alone," she said. "She'll be all right. You wait till she starts high school and blossoms out."

That did it. I looked my father in the eye. "Yes," I said. "I liked it."

Sample's Crossing

His mother drove too fast for the narrow road that dipped off the shadeless hills, sank down through the old cuts, and then snaked ahead, an oiled line across the sagebrush that seemed to be drawing them according to a plan that might change and veer off at any time. She gripped the wheel tightly and peered ahead, squinting into the mirages that evaporated as her car shot toward them, and she kept the needle of the speedometer hovering near the red, as though to overtake the road, to reach her destination in spite of its designs.

He had offered to drive, to let her have a break, but she had said no, at least driving gave her something to keep her thoughts on. Since then, they had not spoken; it was too hot; even the air that flowed into the car through the vents was parched. He could not take a breath shallow enough to keep the fine, filtering dust out of his nose and mouth. Sooner or later, he supposed he would feel something, had been expecting to feel something since yesterday morning, when his roommate had wakened him and said his mother was on the phone. But so far nothing, only a kind of uneasy embarrassment at his mother's grief; and so he leaned back against the sticky vinyl seat and allowed his drowsiness to drag at his eyelids, although he would have supposed sleep, ordinary sleep from which he would wake, would be a kind of betrayal now.

When his eyes jerked open, it was with a sense that the car no longer was hurtling through the scorched pasture land, in fact had been sitting, stalled, for some time. Dismayed, he saw through the open window on his side the edge of the oiled road, soft and reeking under the midday sun, a gravel ditch where bleached weeds grew, and a barbed wire fence holding back miles of waist-high sagebrush. A stench—not road tar, not sage—assaulted him; it was steam, acrid, wet; and he tore himself from the bare August bones of the prairie to see that the hood of the car was up and the vaporizing moisture rolling out.

His mother came around the front of the car in her suit and heels and saw that he was awake. "God damn it," she said.

"What's wrong?"

He opened the door, then found his shoes with his bare feet before stepping out on the tar.

"I don't know!"

He approached the raised hood cautiously, but the steam already was subsiding, so he could look into the engine. Not that he knew much more about it than his mother did, only that it still was sizzling in its depths. Knowing about cars, about the mechanical parts of things and how they worked, never had come as natural insight to him as it seemed to come to other boys his age.

He straightened up from the engine and looked back along the empty road. Hours ago there had been hayfields, and men baling hay, and loaded farm trucks pulling out on the highway, their sunburned drivers waving casually to his mother as though she were someone they knew (and she had waved back, as though she did, indeed, know them, despite her preoccupation.) But here was nothing, only the crippled car and the whir of a grasshopper in the skeletal grass. The horizon shimmered in the heat, fading into sky. One more step backward and the car might fade, too, and he would have stepped out of the machine age.

"—of all times, why now? It's already nearly noon, and the service will be at two—"

If she started to cry, he could not bear it. The void yawned.

"It's probably just the radiator water," he said, out of a desperate cast for a reason to give her.

But his mother snatched for it, her face lightening in relief. "But—if water is all we need—we're less than a mile from the river!"

"How do you know?" he asked, suspicious. He knew she remembered a great deal about the country where she had been brought up, but she had not, after all, been born like his grandfather with a map of the country burned into his memory like a pigeon's instinct.

—and if it were his grandfather he had been traveling with today, he would have had a child's confidence in the old man's knowing his way. Alone, with his loss waiting like the sight of a wound that must be carried to the brain in slow motion before the pain hits, every mile upon mile of sagebrush looked the same.

His mother laughed. The sound jarred the empty grass. "Because I can see it from here! Look!" And she pointed south, in the direction they had been driving.

He turned, squinting against the waves of heat rising off the road. Once he knew where to look, he could see the narrow glint of silver between the cutbanks and the dusty tops of trees. She was right, less than a mile, hardly half a mile away. He tasted the residue of his fear only when he breathed it out.

"We can fetch water. There's a jug in the trunk—" she was unlocking it, lifting out the gallon glass jar.

"Both of us don't have to go," he offered, but he was relieved when she replied,

"No. I'll walk with you. I don't want to sit alone and think."

Once the car was behind them, the sensation of being alone, in slow motion in another time, returned. Nothing was in sight—cutbanks, slopes whitened with alkali, even the bleached and twisted cedar fence posts, the rusting barbed wire—that could not have been in place fifty, a hundred years ago. The sun bore down. It was very quiet. He could hear his own breathing, and the crunch of their footsteps on the fine gravel on the shoulder of the road, and the rustling of some small creature in the sagebrush, getting away unseen.

Even some of his mother's urgency seemed to have drained away with the heat. Once she stopped and pointed.

"Coyote."

He looked at her, not after the coyote, which he could not have seen in the first place, for he lacked the country-bred child's instinctive eye for signs of life in the void.

His mother did not look as though she had that eye. In her white lace blouse and dark plum skirt—at least she'd left the jacket to her suit in the car, folded neatly—she was an exotic on this road, even with her hair floating, even with her face flushed. And yet she

149

knew where she was, after—thirty years, he supposed—living in town. She knew more than he did.

"You should have stayed in the car," he said. "There would have been a little shade, and I could have been to the river and back with water—"

He hoped water was all they needed. Out here on foot, on this road, he felt the inadequacy of his soft skin, his soft white muscles, his lack of any sense of direction. Any barricade between him and the endless glaring space, even the useless shell of the car, would have been better than none.

His mother shrugged, walking, her patent leather heels sinking slightly into the dust with each step. "Oh, probably the Barbours will be home, some of them—your Barbour cousins—I can go inside and visit with Polly and cool off—"

He stopped. "People live out here?"

"Yes, right there by the river."

"Have they lived here long?"

His mother considered his question seriously. "About sixty years, I suppose."

It was the sun, he thought, that left him lightheaded. To be stranded out here, alone with his mother, the sun beating down on their heads, the car broken down, perhaps irremediably—knowing he had no resources, on his own, for survival—and then to learn that this dry, bleached landscape was inhabited after all, and by cousins of his. Yes, now he could see, under the dusty clump of trees on the other side of the river, sheds and a low house. No signs of life, but not deserted, not dead and forgotten like the paintless shacks in the midst of the stubble fields they had driven past earlier.

"I didn't know I had any Barbour cousins."

"Well, second cousins—worse than that, really. I suppose Polly's girls are my second cousins—so their children are your—third? fourth?—my God, it hardly seems worth counting that far. No wonder the family seems to fall apart." She brooded on it. "I guess we just counted cousins in those days. We didn't worry about degrees."

"I never knew any of our family lived out here."

She stared at him. "Oh, yes! Grandpa's—my great-grandfather's—homestead was on this side of Fort Maginnis, and several of his children filed south of the river here. It was Dad that moved north of town."

"I can't imagine you livng anywhere like this," he said.

"It's not so bad. It's only thirty miles from Fort Maginnis by road."

Now he could see the bridge, an ordinary state highway bridge with loose gravel and low concrete guardrails, all the color of dust under the unrelenting sun. Fixed on the outer face of the guardrail was a small white sign, edged in black, with thin block lettering: JUDITH RIVER. He felt as though he had come upon an artifact of the twentieth century.

Across the bridge, not a leaf stirred. "I don't think anybody's home," he said.

"They've probably left for Fort Maginnis already." Her chin jerked, trembled. "I hadn't thought. Of course Polly would go to the funeral. He was her real cousin—first cousin."

"We'll be there. We've got plenty of time!" he said hastily.

"Yes. Yes."

But now she seemed to be in no hurry. She walked to the middle of the bridge and leaned over the guardrail, so far that he took an involuntary step toward her. But her eyes were downstream, where the river shallowed in a bend through the sagebrush and danced over a gravel bar in the sun.

"That's Sample's Crossing," she said without taking her eyes off the current.

So that was it.

The sensation of having been here before, on this exact spot, hearing those exact words, faded almost before he knew he had experienced it. In its place grew a curious desolation that flattened everything in sight.

"You can see it's shallow enough there to ford with a band of sheep," she said.

He realized he never had expected to hear the name, Sample's Crossing, spoken aloud again; he had supposed, without conscious thought, that now his grandfather was gone, the name would linger, a mute ghost, in some minor convolution of his own brain.

151

But it meant something, Sample's Crossing, more than the name, he couldn't remember what. He never before had known exactly where it was, never had heard anyone but his grandfather call it by that name. One of the old-timers' place-names, he thought, lost or about to be lost like dozens, hundreds more that hadn't made it on the state highway maps or the official black-edged signs. Every gulch, every draw in the country had had its own name, once—the Christie Hill, the Greasenour Cut-Off, the Bohemian Flats—mere echoes to him, to whom there were no landmarks.

"Who was Sample?" he asked.

"Oh—he homesteaded here. Jess was his son."

He felt dizzy again. "We'd better find water," he said.

Across the bridge a few trees, willows and scabby cottonwoods, cast shade over a yard of packed dirt and a patch of hollyhocks growing along a board fence. The house was one storey, painted white, foundationless, with a porch built flush with the ground. Narrow sashed windows looked through a straggling vine.

Careful of her nylon stockings, his mother pushed open the board-and-wire gate and walked along the plank to the porch.

"Nobody's home," he warned, slowing his walk. His neck was prickling with the feeling that he was a trespasser.

A sign of life; an old dog, raising his head from his bed of gunny sacks in the shade of the porch.

"Hello, Ring," she said, and his tail thumped on the warped boards.

"How do you know his name?"

"What? Oh—maybe it isn't his name. Ring is what they used to call all the ring-necked sheepdogs."

She was trying the door.

"Mother," he said. "You can't just walk into somebody else's house. We can get water from the river."

But the knob was turning, the door swinging open. Uneasily he followed her into a small dim room.

After the glare of the sun on the flats it seemed blessedly cool. As his eyes adjusted to the light, he made out furniture—an old couch covered with a blanket, a plastic lampstand, an upright piano loaded with photographs—and a door opening on a kitchen of sorts; the corner of a table, covered with oilcloth, a sink with a cotton curtain on a drawstring hiding its pipes.

Without hesitating, as though she knew her way, his mother went into the kitchen with her jar. In a moment he heard water running.

Feeling like a voyeur who might be apprehended at any minute, he wandered over to the piano and looked at the photographs. Faces of all ages looked back, from cracked and faded brown prints, from black-and-white glossies, from modern colored snapshots. Children, dogs, sheep, family groups in stiff lines, young men who, forty or fifty years ago, might have been his age—he scanned their features for any resemblance to himself and found none.

Something damp touched his hand; it was the old dog, thrusting with its nose. He bent to pat the thickened head and got a whiff of its foetid odor. "Ugh—damn, go back outside!"

But the old dog only wagged its tail. He saw its eyes were filmed over with a white rheum, and he moved away himself.

If his mother had married and settled down in a place like this—but she had not; she had rebelled as a young girl and gone her own way, and therefore he had not had to. Otherwise he might have been, he supposed, one of the boys in the fields, hauling thirty tons of baled hay out on the highway—but no. There had been words at the time of his mother's going, he believed. Not an outright quarrel with her parents, but hard feelings because of her choice, and so she had seldom returned, and then only because of him, the grandson.

Had he—the image blurred, receding, just out of reach—ridden, as a small boy, in the cab of his grandfather's truck as the old man drove over this road? The sprung seat in the old Dodge, the layers of padding working out from the tear in the leather, the junk on the floor, a bale of twine rolling around, the bucket of blackened spare parts under his feet—all clear enough, but from that or from other journeys? Had his grandfather stopped here, right here, pointed to the crossing, and said—but it was gone.

"Strange, memory."

He jumped; he had not heard her come up behind him. She was

gazing at the photographs, her eyes miles away, the gallon jar of water balanced in her arms.

"They say nothing is ever really forgotten. It submerges somewhere in the brain. Like a computer program, waiting for something to stimulate the memory, bring it to the surface—"

"I always think of that when I'm writing an exam," he said, trying to joke.

"Dad would have known all these people. Who they married, what they named their children—oh, maybe Polly knows, but when she goes, and she'll be next—" his mother shrugged. "Faces without names, that's all."

"Do you know any of them?"

"A few." She indicated one or two, naming them, with names that meant nothing to him.

Did she have regrets, now?—behind that clear, sad face, kept to herself along with her grief?—No, he told himself, she couldn't; couldn't regret these entombed faces, this narrow dim room, the dust. And outside, the empty miles of sun glaring on the rocks, pressing down—almost, he could believe the walls were moving closer, pressing against his shoulders; and his spine tingled with the premonition.

The old dog had padded up, nuzzling her skirt. "Go away, Ring," she said absently. "You smell bad."

Something stirred. "Who was Jess Sample?"

"What?" His mother stared at him, her face as pale and strained as though she were trying to hear his voice over a passage of miles. "Jess? He was a sheepherder."

"But there's more," he insisted. "Who was he?"

Her eyes dropped to the uncovered jar of water in her arms. The water had its own smell, gaseous, alkali. Fine streams of bubbles laced the glass. Slowly, as though reading the words in the water, his mother added, "He was born here—near here. He wanted to marry Aunt Maria—Polly's mother—and he built this house for her, but she married someone else. Years later, when Polly ran off and married Jake—she was only fifteen—Maria bought her this house to live in."

He waited in her silence, watching her face as she relived it; the story had a meaning for her, but it was not the one he sought. "There must be more!" he burst. "Something to do with Granddad!"

"No-o." She was shaking her head, bewildered. "Oh, as a young man, Dad knew Jess. He—"

"Yes?"

"He was one of Jess's pallbearers."

"Go on!" He was willing the words out of her, straining them, for what he was not sure.

"But there's nothing more!" she protested.

"But there is! Something to do with Granddad!"

"Jess was murdered," she said. Her voice made it a question: is that what it is? what you were trying to remember? When he said nothing, she went on. "He was shot to death while guarding the lamb band, miles from anywhere, and they never knew who did it."

Their eyes met.

"When I was a girl, I thought it was the most romantic story," she said. "And when I was in college, I even wrote a story about Jess and Maria—and in my story, he died because of her—a kind of suicide. But it wasn't really that way."

"It meant something to Granddad. Jess's story. I know it did."

"I'm sorry," she said. "I don't remember any more. I really don't."

He turned away in frustration. The walls met him, blank; and in a room full of something to lose, he was again the voyeur, eternally unattached and floating.

"Dad would have known," she said. "I'm sorry."

"We'd better go back to the car," he said, "and see if water is what it needs."

"If I could have—at least come home oftener, brought you home, you might have developed a sense of the family—had a sense of place—but for me, for him, it had to be all one or all the other, I don't know why—and it isn't as though I've done so much with my life, after all. When you compare me with Polly—what does it come to?"

"We'd better go," he said. "We don't belong here."

155

He closed Polly's door behind them as his mother, carrying the jar of water in her arms, crossed the sagging porch and walked along the plank, her heels tap-tapping. The old dog made as though to follow them but stopped at the gate and sat on his haunches in the dust, turning his head after them as though his white eyes could see them leave.

"I could carry that," he said. He felt relieved; they had walked in and out without being caught.

"No."

Once out of the shade of the trees, the sun burst upon them, a blow of clarity, dazzling on the old river crossing and whitening the road and the bridge. A little water had sloshed out of the jar, seeping down his mother's skirt in a dark line against the plum, briefly dark against the dust; and then his mother's slim figure wavered, blurred; and, slicing through his relief, an amputation as clean as the line between sun and shadow, he saw the sum total of his grandfather's memory ebbing, like a tape unwinding, slower and slower, the end flapping, disconnected; and at long last, he understood his loss.

Last Night
As I Lay
On the Prairie

Here in the smaller communities, where the surrounding plains seem endless, and the clouds rolling across the open blue so vast that theirs might be the only shadows, it is easy to forget that one culture is rapidly replacing another. In a town that grew over an old Metis settlement along a creek bottom, a generation of transplanted cottonwoods has had time to grow, decay, and cast shade and a litter of fluff and dead twigs over the sidewalks and the seedy lawns and the front porches. And in the neighborhoods of two-story frame houses which seem impervious to the inroads of the new four-lane highway and quick food joints and car lots and shopping malls, indifferent to the new bare housing developments cropping up on the unsheltered slopes above town, it still is the custom to bring food to the homes of the recently bereaved.

Plates and plates of food. Tableloads of food over which the family and friends gather after the services in decorum or shock or curiosity or relief, to eat of the communally prepared food as though it might contain the power to embalm them against the trespasses of their own mortality.

And so it comes about that, over the funeral baked ham, my mother finds the opportunity to ask me for the fourth time whether she ever told me that my father had found out who murdered Jess Sample.

Trapped, with all possibility of escape cut off, I glare at her over my dripping plate of salad. In decency I cannot turn my back on her and howl that nobody has cared in fifty years who killed Jess Sample, it has mattered to no one, it has made no difference under the sun. But I cannot scream at her, certainly not here in the living room of the decent inlaws. The most I can do is grate it out:

"Yes. You did mention that."

"Oh." She hesitates, confused. "I did tell you, then?"

159

"Yes."

But she has no mercy for me. Here in this suffocating dim living room, crowded with plastic madonnas and second cousins, thick with the smell of cooked food and the murmurous platitudes of three generations, my mother intends to tell me the story all over again. She wets her lips, about to begin.

Then, unexpectedly, I am saved by my cousin Buck in his good dark suit, coming up to put his arm around me.

"Juley, how've you been?"

"Fine, thank you," I assure him gratefully, and see my mother turn away, dazed, with her paper plate sagging under its load of food.

"That boy of yours! I hardly knew him. Grew up overnight, didn't he?"

"It seemed like it."

"Been a hell of a summer. Hay's burning up in the fields and I ought to be out swathing it right now, but then this comes along, and the least I can do for John—"

It is less Buck's face than his hands that have altered. After all, he has been ranching for a living, a living in more than one sense of the word, none of which my son and his friends would comprehend. For children do not play in irrigation ditches together forever, and Buck's hand on my shoulder has become an adult male's, the skin grown leathery and cracked, the nails horny, a durable hand shaped to grip and lift, although pallbearers nowadays need not bear the physical weight of a casket.

—When you're asked to serve as a pallbearer, you answer that you'd be greatly honored, explained my father.

("Do I have to?" complained my son when I telephoned him. "It isn't like it means anything. Or that he'll be there to appreciate it.")

—Have you been a pallbearer often? I asked my father.

—Once for Uncle Theo. Once for Jess Sample. This time—

That time, I remember, it had been for Aunt Maria, and I had been eighteen and self-consciously sad about the passing of the earliest generation I knew.

"Buck—" I begin, impulsively, for he is Aunt Maria's grandson, two years younger than I, but well able to remember a time when they were mostly all still alive and one death counted for little. And now it has been Buck's turn to leave his hay drying to tinder in the field while he dresses in his dark suit and necktie and does the decent thing.

But Buck and I have no words in common. Although his face is familiar, with the pale blue eyes, slightly protruberant, that mark all the cousins, and the long Ware mouth, he no longer really is Buck, my cohort in a hundred childish enterprises. Already he is edging away.

"We're all very grateful to you," I end by saying, and he nods, embarrassed to be thanked. When I look again he has walked off to stand with his wife across the room, his back turned, a head taller than the rest of the crowd around the dining room table, his neck sunburned and vulnerable above his white shirt collar.

Perhaps after all I don't want to talk to Buck or to any of them. For the first time all afternoon I am alone for a moment, temporarily stranded from the crowd like a river island when the current briefly divides around the bare sand. I begin to feel myself again. No, I have nothing to say to any of these people, have no wish to see a ghost reflected in the eyes I meet. I chose to leave this place too long ago, wanted never to set foot in a room like this one again, and now I have raised a son to whom all this is inexplicable.

It is long and narrow, a small living room and a small dining room thrown together. Varnished dark wainscoting and tight single-sashed windows, their shades drawn against the dust from the unpaved street and the rumble of traffic on the way out of town. Couches and chairs pushed back against the walls to make space for the oak table with all its leaves added.

Ham and rolls and preserves and Pyrex dishes full of jello salads and dripping coleslaw and congealing casseroles and pans of baked beans and fried chicken and relishes and pies and cakes. More food than all of us possibly can eat, even this crowd—for it was one of the most crowded funerals anyone has seen, with all the seats taken by the early comers, and old friends, old neighbors from Coffee Creek days waiting on the sidewalks outside the funeral parlor for their chance to file past the casket—waiting in the dust the wind whipped across Main Street, the women in their summer dresses, the men in their good clean clothes and their hats in their weatherbeaten hands, one old fellow in an aluminum walker, barely able to drag himself up the aisle to the casket.

To keep from remembering the old man in the walker and the look on his face as he struggled with it, I turn to the pictures on the walls around me, where the Old West lives on in the midst of the crucifixes and the plaster saints.

We had these pictures on our walls, too. The Parrish prints of the lone wolf and the melancholy Indian maiden. The C.M. Russell prints celebrating in authentic detail the cattle drive and the horse thieves and the last stand. Original oils, also of cattle drives and last stands. These last I can hardly bear to face; they are too much like my own teenaged efforts.

How proud my father was of my artwork. I had to go off to college to find out how rotten I really was.

—She got the cabin just right. Just the way it was. And the man in the door, just the way Jess used to stand and watch me ride into sight—

—And did Jess always know it was you? I pressed him, knowing the answer, wanting to hear it again.

—Only fooled him once, and that was when I was breaking that stocking-legged sorrel colt for Kate Melloy. I could see Jess kinda peer and peer out his door as I rode down the hill on that colt, and finally I got close enough I could see he'd busted out in a grin. Thought it was you, he said. Just couldn't figure out that fancy stocking-legged outfit you're riding.

—So Jess always knew who it was by the horse whoever was riding?

—He could recognize the horse by his gait and his build further off than he could the man. But he could recognize the man just by the way he sat his saddle. Told you, didn't I, about the first time Jess ever saw me?

And even this afternoon, in this ghastly narrow room of hushed talk and the smell of cooling food, I remember how I nodded, eager to hear the story again.

—I'd ridden over to Aunt Maria's for some reason. Maybe just to pick up the mail. I was riding old Midge. She was a

three-year-old that spring. And you know how the road used to
run all the way down that long hill to the house?

—Yes, I nodded.

—All the way down the hill, I could see they were sitting on the
front porch and watching me. And when I finally rode up to the
yard fence, Aunt Maria came out to meet me, kinda laughing. This
is Jess Sample, she said. Do you know what Jess wanted to know
when you rode in sight? He watched you for a little while, and then
he said, Maria, did your brother John ever have a boy? Because if
he did, that's his boy riding down that hill right now. Couldn't
nobody else but John's own boy sit a horse like that.

—And that was the first time you ever met Jess? I asked.

—I'd knowed who he was for years, of course, but it was the
winter after that I stayed out of high school and camped with him
while I ran the trapline, and then I stayed and helped him through
lambing time—

And now here are these paintings, naive in perspective and
peculiar in the drawing, but exact in their rendering of the details of
chaps and boots and pigging strings and the rigging of saddles, the
slant of the shoulders as the cowboy takes his dallies, the shift in
balance as he throws his weight upon the opposing stirrup against
the weight of the steer hitting the end of the lariat. Specific and
faithful, a celebration of the least detail of a twilight world.

A tap on my shoulder. My mother, breathing heavily from the
chase, has cornered me again.

"So much food. So many people that cared so much about your
dad."

"Yes."

"Did you notice the Lucases? And did you notice Eldon Stanford
came? He had to drive all the way down from Hayes this morning.
And did you happen to notice Art Simmons?"

A full revolution of memory tells me what I had known all along
but refused to recognize. Art Simmons, horse-breaker from the
lower Judith with his big rope-burned hands, playing the piano
after dinner with his three remaining fingers, winking at the little
girl who watched him from under the table, was the old man dragging himself up the aisle in his walker today.

"By the way. Did I think to tell you? Did you know your dad found out who killed Jess Sample?"

It doesn't matter! I want to scream. *Who cares who killed Jess Sample?* But I answer her quietly, "Yes, you did," and she blinks in bewilderment. For a moment I see her as though she were a stranger: a small graying woman with sunburned face and arms, her eyes so blurred with the past that she is oblivious to much of the present.

"I meant to tell Art. But he's so hard of hearing now, and I didn't want to shout it so loud, with so many standing around—"

No, she wouldn't want to shout such news in front of others. Not that her story could be called confidential, exactly, after fifty years. But at the time, it was a local sensation, an unsolved murder, or, at least, an unsatisfactorily solved one.

—They tried young Walsh for it, and they even had him in the pen a couple of years, but they was just looking for somebody to nail it to. Nobody ever believed Walsh done it.

—No one ever admitted to it?

—Never did.

—But what was the motive? There had to be a motive! I insisted.

And then I waited through the long pause, watching my father's face, knowing that after all those years he still was sifting through layers of impressions, details, fragments, in search of pattern.

—They never was sure. At Walsh's trial they made out that Jess might of been stealing grass for his sheep, and hell, I wouldn't of put it past Jess, not if his sheep was hungry. Jess was one of your true old-timers, and with them old boys, their stock always come first.

My father paused again—Jess would of died for his sheep, all right, he said.

And how, I now wonder, in this dusty afternoon, in this narrow oasis within sound of the new highway construction, within smelling distance of the hot asphalt they are pouring, would Jess's story sound? As heard, say, through my son's ears? Remote, primitive? Or merely boring? He and his friends take false arrest and imprisonment for granted, assume entrapment is commonplace and all motives base.

My mother wets her lips and starts. "Your dad was drinking coffee in town one day when a young fellow came up to him and said, 'You're John Ware, aren't you?' And then he told him what his father's name had been, but—"

But his father was dead now, and his uncle was dead, and he kind of thought John Ware ought to know the whole story, being there was nobody still alive it could hurt, says my mind, running ahead with the narrative. But before my mother can repeat it out loud, I am saved again, this time by my sister Lou.

Lou's eyes contain a dangerous glitter. "We've got to do something with these chrysanthemums," she says.

"Chrysanthemums?" My mother looks bewildered. "What became of them all?"

"These are the potted plants. Nine of them. We had all the cut flowers sent up to the hospital."

"Oh."

"I thought we could send a plant home with Polly. And leave one or two here for Celia."

"Celia—yes, she would enjoy a plant. So good of her to open her home for us like this—Celia!" And spying her, my mother darts off.

Empty space is all that separates Lou and me. Uneasily, we meet each other's eyes.

"I don't suppose *you* want to take a plant home with you?"

"No! No—it's three hundred miles, and there's so much packed in the car already, and it's so hot—"

I break off, seeing my hasty defenses as in a mirror, in the face so much like my own. My sister, my old enemy. The one who stayed home, who jealously guarded her frontiers against my ever returning until her gradual realization that I never wanted to come back.

As if in acknowledgement, she shrugs. "Somebody has to take care of things."

True, and in our family, Lou is the one the task has fallen to. Lou, dry-eyed, who made the late-night phone calls and listened while the conventional protests dwindled into silence, then asked the necessary questions: when can you get here, is Thursday too soon?—Friday afternoon, then, or would it be better to wait until

Monday? Lou who made the practical arrangements. The casket, the gravesite, the reception. Even the gist of the sermon. Even the disposal of the chrysanthemums. Now her eye holds mine, daring me to carp.

"Lou, I know this hasn't been easy for you—"

But she draws back, and again I have the sensation of seeing two women at once, like a double exposure; Lou, *Lou*, my sister, flesh almost as familiar as my own, but superimposed upon a frowning tired stranger, dressed like any ranch wife, with wrists and stomach and thighs thickened by hard work and a starchy diet. What to say next to this woman?

"The last few years were hard on him," Lou says. "Everything is so changed. Even the wheat diseases are different. He couldn't keep up."

"Did he ever tell you about Jess Sample and the man in the coffee shop?"

"Only fifty or sixty times," she says wearily. "He got to where he lived more and more in the past. But now—" And suddenly her face lightens as she tells me about modern production charts, modern mechanization, ratios of chemicals to yields, moisture conservation. "Farming's a business now, it's dangerous to believe it isn't. That's where Buck made his mistake. That's why they're foreclosing. Can you believe he's still irrigating with ditches and diverting his water by hand?"

"Foreclosing. You mean he's losing the ranch? But that's Aunt Maria's old homestead!"

"It's going to be hard on him," Lou concedes. "But he can't live in the past."

"No. Of course not."

Lou goes off on a diatribe against government support programs, the prime rate of interest, the record numbers of farm foreclosures over the past few years, but I stop listening. Farm. The very word sounds flat. Ranch, that was the word we were brought up to say.

"At least it's over and done with. Thank God for that," Lou startles me by saying. Then I realize she means the funeral.

"Yes," I agree.

"Are you driving back tonight?"

"I suppose so. David will be eager to get back."

"He'll graduate next spring? It must seem strange to you." And again I wonder what she means. "Yes," I agree.

"Well—" Lou shrugs, then squints as the deepening afternoon sunlight blinds her with a bolt shot from under the drawn shades. The light falls over her shoulder to saturate the muddy colors of the oil paintings. For just a moment they are infused with an illusion of life; the tiny cowboys sit tense in their saddles, their cattle glow in their natural reds and buffs, and their shadows fall on dry dust and sage.

Only a moment, and the illusion fades. I turn and face my mother.

"—He told your dad his family had always known. It was his uncle. His uncle was the kind that would do anything, for no reason. One night—he remembered it himself, he was a little boy at the time—his uncle rode in and told them, I just shot that Scotch sheepherder. They all knew what his uncle was. But they never told. I—I was going to tell Art Simmons, but Art is so hard of hearing, and anyway I can't think of the man's name. Your dad told me what it was, but—I just can't—"

Unbidden comes the spectacle of my mother shouting in the ear of a deaf man the story of a fifty-year-old murder, perpetrated by a man whose name she cannot remember. I would like to laugh, but my father told me the story, too, last summer when I drove down for a day, and I can't remember the name either.

A breath of air is what I need. Even hot September air, permeated with the odor of asphalt. My feet are carrying me toward the front porch, into the pale full daylight of an early fall evening, where a slight rustle of cottonwood leaves makes me hear the rumble of traffic I normally would have blotted out.

Alone and settling into myself again, my mind begins out of habit to tick off its chores. A few odds and ends to pack, the long drive, home by midnight if I'm fortunate. David to see off in the morning, then the draft for the foundation to finish by noon. The threads of routine, the underpinnings of my life. So much to do, so little time.

From blocks away sound the whine of tires and a car accelerating with a shriek of young voices. Teenagers, out cruising the loop, oblivious to life outside their metal shells. I begin to cast Jess Sample's story as I would try to tell it to David on the drive home—the slightly ironical tone, humorous even, that I might use to catch his interest. But I know I might as well run down the street and shout it after the kids in their speeding rattletraps.

I never will know who shot Jess Sample. The tenuous threads my mother has drawn from his story and tried to hand to me—there, now, is another matter; a matter of those who will do anything for no reason, and those who insist on a motive. And I shiver in spite of the lingering heat, because already it is September, and the cottonwood leaves are rustling toward a conclusion.

The Snowies,
the Judiths

A knock came at the door, and all eyes rose from the lesson. Mrs. Trask, looking troubled at yet another distraction, laid her book face down on the rules regarding *ser* and *estar* and went to answer it. Her first try at opening the door, however, met resistance. Had the knocker forgotten that the classroom doors opened outward into the corridor, or had he changed his mind about delivering his message, or was he merely being funny?

The students snickered, and Mrs. Trask flushed. It was hard enough for a substitute teacher to contain their excess energy during tournament season, let alone pretend to teach a lesson, without pranksters in the hall. She wrenched hard at the knob just as its resistance gave way.

The door opened so violently that the students saw Mrs. Trask lurch and almost lose her footing. Then she was taking a fast step back into the classroom. Her feet, however, in her new high heeled shoes were far from fast enough to balance the backward propulsion of her body. She landed on her back, her head bumping against the glazed oak floor. Her feet scrabbled frantically out of her shoes, as though in search of some small lost possession of great value, while her torso bucked and thrust in such a familiar and explicit way that some of the students laughed outright. But the most surprising thing about Mrs. Trask was the red flower that bloomed where her face had been, bloomed and pulsed and overflowed its petals on the oak.

Mary Dare in the back row had put her fingers in her ears to stop the vibrations. Now she took her hands away, because she knew what made ears ring the way hers were ringing. She recognized the whine and crack, too, that had run like lightning around the edges of the explosion. Impossible to mistake those sounds. Only last weekend her father had let her fire a round with the .44, and her first shot had ricocheted off sandstone and whined. What she did not recognize, never had heard before in her life, were the stacatto pips and shrills and squeals—well, yes, they did remind her of waking suddenly at night to the yammer of coyote pups, a pack of fools as her father called them, rallying for the first time in their lives with thin immature yips that chilled her and yet drew her out of her warm sleep to imagine herself walking with them through the cutbanks in the dark—the sounds that were rising now outside the classroom door and down the corridor as more shots reverberated.

Mary Dare stood up, thinking to see and perhaps comprehend. Then Ryan Novotny tackled her, big Ryan who as a senior really shouldn't have been in the first-year Spanish class at all but sat beside Mary Dare so he could copy her answers. Mary Dare found herself lying on her back between two rows of desks, looking up at the fluorescent lights burning away.

"Ho*ly*, Ryan," she said.

"Get down! Get down!" Ryan was yelling. "You crazy bastards, get your heads down!"

Now Ryan was crawling up the aisle next to hers on his elbows and knees. His rear end in his 501's was higher than his shoulders, and Mary Dare wanted to laugh at the sight he made. Somebody in the front of the room was laughing. Or hiccoughing, one or the other.

Mary Dare rolled over on her belly, wishing she hadn't worn her good white cotton sweater and jeans. She crawled below the surfaces of desks, as Ryan had done, over trails of dust and forgotten pencils and past crouching people's feet in shoes she recognized but never had expected to see at eye level. She crawled until she reached Jennifer Petty and took her hand and felt Jennifer's fingers lock on to hers while Jennifer went on hiccoughing and snuffling. Mary Dare lay with something, she thought a Spanish book, digging into her shoulder and her fingers in Jennifer's slippery grip. She could see the dark underside of Jennifer's desk, wafered with petrified discs of gum, and the pilling red dacron mountain that was Jennifer in her awful sweater from Bonanza, and the inside of

Jennifer's fat white wrist so close to Mary Dare's face that Mary Dare barely could bring her eyes to focus on individual freckles. Not a hand Mary Dare normally would be holding. Jennifer was weird. Jennifer's fingers kept slipping almost out of hers, but at the last second Jennifer would grab on again, so tight that Mary Dare could see her own fingers turning as white as Jennifer's, with tiny red lines seeping out between them and crawling down her wrist into the sleeve of her sweater.

Mary Dare arched her back to ease it off the cutting edge of the book or whatever she was lying on and settled down to wait for Ryan. Nothing would happen until Ryan came back. Ryan would be her early warning system. Mary Dare reduced the disgusting underside of Jennifer's desk to a blur by focusing on the ceiling light and letting all thought escape her. Nothing ever had happened to her, nothing ever would again. Fighting this morning with Amy and her mother over the hair dryer or Amy's endless sappy Bon Jovi tapes, guarding her painfully acquired collection of cosmetics and her really nice sweaters, getting on the school bus this morning in the dark, looking forward to getting out of classes early for the basketball tournament—none of it existed. All was reduced to the pain in her back, and Jennifer's grip in hers, and the light endlessly burning.

A shadow grew over the mountain of Jennifer, thrusting its head between Mary Dare and the light. Mary Dare blinked, and the shadow took form as Ryan.

"I can't see nothing. It's crazy out there."

Mary Dare pulled back from the brink with regret. Lint stuck in Ryan's hair and rolls of dust tracked his sweater. She felt bored with the sight of him, then sick. She rolled up on her elbow, tentatively. The line of windows was too high for her on the floor to see anything of the world outside except the fading February daylight and the distant tips of the mountains, snow-capped. For a moment she almost could breathe the freezing clean air of escape, almost feel the snow on her ankles as she ran.

"Forget it," Ryan whispered. "Them windows don't open. The bastards must of thought they was building a fucking jail when they built this place."

"Could you see him?" came a whisper behind Mary Dare.

"No, shit, couldn't see anything. I couldn't get far. All those doors and halls. He bagged Zeidel, though. I could see that."

Mary Dare closed her eyes. Ten feet away, on the other side of their wall, was the main corridor leading to the school offices. Lined with lockers, interspersed with classroom doors. After the utility dark greens and high ceilings of the old high school, the new doors painted in blues and violets had zinged at her for about the first week of school before they subsided into a familiarity as invisible as the soles of her feet.

The corridor had taken back its substance now, though. She could feel it through the wall.

"Always knew it would happen," Ryan was complaining. "Always knew it, always knew they'd pen us up like this and then take shots at us—"

"You're *paranoid*, Ryan," Mary Dare said. But she understood what he meant. She too, always had known somehow that it would come to this: the closed room, the graying windows, herself and all her classmates huddled under their desks, none daring to raise their heads while they waited for the inevitable next act. It was as though she had dreamed a thousand times about every detail. The hardwood floor, the dark underside of the desk, her knees drawn up, her arms wrapped around her skull; dreamed so many times, become so familiar that she no longer saw nor felt nor was aware of it, until now, by daylight, she recognized it at once. It was the end she always had known was coming, *and now that it's here*, unexpectedly rose her innermost voice, *we might as well get on with it.*

"Hey! Ryan! Town-ass!"

"What?" hissed Ryan.

It was Tom Barnes. She could see the blue flowered sleeve of his cowboy shirt; she remembered he usually sat in front.

"Could you see Zeidel?"

"Hell, yes. He was down. I could tell it was him by his suit." Tom reared up on his elbows. "Oh shit, your arm."

"Yeh, her arm. And she calls me paranoid. Just because they're out to get us doesn't mean—"

Now that she was reminded of it, Mary Dare remembered how warm and wet her wrist and forearm felt. She glanced along the line of her sleeve and saw the sodden dark cuff of her white sweater and her red glistening fingers locked in Jennifer's.

"I don't think it's me," said Mary Dare. "It must be Jennifer."

To roll out from under Jennifer's desk, she was going to have to let go of Jennifer's hand. Testing, Mary Dare relaxed her fingers and felt a flutter of protest.

"Don't cry," Ryan pleaded.

"I *wasn't*," said Mary Dare. "Oh, you mean her."

Mary Dare dug the heels of her hightops into the floor and arched her back much as Mrs. Trask had done. By squirming on her shoulders and inching herself along with her heels, she got her head clear of Jennifer's desk and rolled over and sat up without quite pulling her fingers out of Jennifer's. She glanced around. Although the desks were more or less in their rows, even with books still open at the assignment, nothing seemed quite in its usual place or even in its usual shape or color.

"Get your head *down!*"

"Hell, he ain't after us," said Tom.

With her free hand Mary Dare probed the mess of red sweater and ploughed red flesh and found the pressure point in Jennifer's arm right where in health class they had said it would be. She bore down through the fat until she felt bone. The depth of her fingers brought Jennifer's eyes popping open.

"I'm sorry," Jennifer whimpered.

"What are you sorry about?" Mary Dare asked her, fascinated.

Jennifer's eyes met Mary Dare's. Mary Dare watched the tip of Jennifer's tongue run around her lips as though she was about to explain herself.

"What makes you so sure?" Ryan was arguing.

Tom Barnes squatted in the aisle in his blue flowered shirt with the pearl snap pockets and his cowboy boots with the genuine undershot heels that had to be specially ordered. "I seen him. He ain't after us."

"Who was he?" Mary Dare wanted to know.

Ryan glared at Tom. Mary Dare, caught between them, looked

from one to the other. Ryan the town-ass, really massive, as the kids here still were saying, and little Tom who wasn't embarrassed by wearing his team roping jacket to high school.

"Then how come she's laying here bleeding?" insisted Ryan.

"Hell, he was aiming at Trask, not us."

"You're being pretty fucking cool about it. For a goat roper. How come she's bleeding?"

He was glaring at Tom, as urgent as if his being called massive by everyone hung on Tom's answer. Mary Dare knew he had no idea that in Portland they wouldn't call him anything. Or Tom either, for that matter. They wouldn't know what to *do* with Tom in Portland. She never had heard of goat ropers until she moved back to Montana.

"Are you trying to tell me that ain't a fucking gunshot wound in her arm?"

"He just flung in a couple extra shots to keep us out of his way," said Tom. "He ain't after us. Petty probably just caught a ricochet."

Tom hunkered forward on his precious boot heels. Watching, Mary Dare understood what he was doing, finally understood what her dad had meant when he caught her horse for the third time last weekend and then advised her to cowboy up. It was amazing. Tom Barnes had cowboyed up.

He studied Jennifer Petty's glistening face and the raw red crater in her arm where Mary Dare was pinching off the spurt of blood. "She ain't going to die of that," he said.

"Who *was* it?" Mary Dare persisted.

"I don't know his name, but he's a kid. I've seen him around."

"I know him," came a whisper from under another of the front desks. "I mean, I seen him around, too. I don't know his name, either."

"You're saying he's after them," said Ryan.

"Well, he got Trask," said Tom Barnes. "And you say he got Zeidel."

"I said Zeidel was down."

Ryan's face worked to contain the idea of being incidental. He was on the verge of tears, Mary Dare realized; she never had seen a boy's tears before, and she didn't want to look at Ryan's, so she shut her eyes.

"Wonder where he went?" came from the whisperer.

"Or if he lost his nerve," said Tom.

Mary Dare heard Ryan snuffle hard against his arm. At least the cowboy was keeping his nerve. The floor was grinding into her hip. She remembered the pine floors in the old high school. Softwood boards, varnished a dark brown that wore away by the spring of every year, hollow as the palms of hands from receiving the feet of generations of students. Floors trodden by her uncles in turn, all of them probably wearing boots like Tom's with undershot heels, and then her dad in his turn. This year should have been Mary Dare's turn. One of the reasons her dad had wanted to move back from the west coast was so that Mary Dare and Amy could ride a school bus down the gulch into the shelter of the mountains, the way he had, and go to the old high school with kids like Tom Barnes. Her dad had recited the names of the mountains, the Snowies, the Judiths, the North Moccasins, the South Moccasins, like charms against any counterarguments her mother could raise, like the fine strings program and the languages program for the girls at Santa Angela High School. Charms for safety, the Snowies, the Judiths, the North Moccasins, the South Moccasions. Snow-capped blue mounds that ringed the town and that had offered a haven even in the long ago days before there was a town and the Blackfeet had ridden down from the north to hunt and raid the Crows. The Snowies, the Judiths, the North Moccasins, the South Moccasins, charms against this moment which, she suddenly understood, her father too must have dreamed a thousand times.

But instead of haven there was the new high school with its low maze of corridors, built and paid for by a levy her parents and the parents of practically every ranch kid she knew had voted against. The old high school wasn't even there any more. On the square block on Water Street was only an empty crater. Little kids had howled in glee when the wrecking ball had knocked its bricks to rubble, its soft floors to splinters. The charm had not worked, the moment had come when she and probably Amy had had to crouch under the futile shelter of their desks in spite of anything her parents or anyone's parents could have done to avert it, the only difference between the dream and waking reality being that another kid, apparently, had pulled the trigger.

And now Mary Dare opened her eyes and met the frozen, astonished eyes of a man in a dark brown uniform with his revolver out.

In the glazed moment in front of the revolver, Mary Dare could remember only the necessity of keeping her fingers down hard on Jennifer's arm until the very end. Then she saw the man's lips move and found with surprise that she could hear what he was saying; in fact, his tone seemed unnecessarily loud, even distorted by volume.

"Oh shit no," he was saying.

It's not me that's bleeding but still alive, it's Jennifer, she thought to answer, but she could not be sure he understood her or even heard her or, although his eyes were fixed on her, even saw her. The others were rising beside her, around her. She could sense their slow unfolding, arms releasing their holds, tentative white faces emerging from under desks. Faces she could name, Tom Barnes and Ryan and Valier and Shannon and Stephen and Michael S. and Tyler and Michael J. and Ashley and Amber, like faces out of the dream, drained of life, all sockets and bones. And then, as they silently rose together, staring across the gulf at the patrolman, he seemed to recognize them with a start. He reholstered his gun.

"We'll get you out of here," his voice boomed and ebbed. He looked from face to face, then wet his lips. "Don't worry, we'll get you out of here."

"I can't let go of Jennifer," whispered Mary Dare. She felt glued to her.

"Somebody say he got another one?"

A sheriff's deputy in a tan gabardine jacket and a gray Stetson stuck his head in the door. His gaze wandered over Mary Dare and he started to say something else. Then his gaze fell to the floor and riveted there. Other men crowded the doorway behind him, vanished, reappeared. More highway patrolmen in dark brown, city policemen in navy blue. Mary Dare saw how their eyes, too, fell first to the floor and then rose in slow surmise to her face and the other faces in the room.

Ryan nudged her, more himself. "Looks like they got all the fuzz in Montana here."

"Something here you'll have to walk by," said the patrolman. "But you don't have to look."

"I can't let go," said Mary Dare. She could feel her own pulse in her fingertips and, faintly, Jennifer's. As long as she held on to Jennifer, she could put off the walk back into the ordinary.

But men were everywhere, all the fuzz in Montana, shoving through the rows of desks, kneeling beside her, their voices thundering at Jennifer while their fingers replaced Mary Dare's in Jennifer's wound. A draught streamed over her warm sticky fingers. She was being lifted by her elbows, steadied on her feet. "You done fine, little girl. We'll take care of her now."

One of the navy blue policemen had brought in a plastic pouch of yellowish fluid and was holding it above his head. A tube dangled down from it. Noise seemed amplified; Mary Dare wanted to yell at Amy to turn down the tape. She saw Jennifer being lifted on a stretcher with a needle taped into the fat part of her arm. The policeman with the pouch and the tube followed her. Mary Dare took a step after her, as toward her last link with flesh and blood, but hands held her back and a voice flexed and roared like a distorted cassette tape over her head: "She'll be all right. Now we're gonna get you out of here."

The floor felt unstable under her, the way the ground felt after a long horseback ride. Mary Dare wobbled toward the door. She knew the others were following her in a shaky line, Valier and Shannon and Stephen and Michael S. and Tyler and Michael J. and Ashley and Amber and everybody. Police on both sides were guiding the line, not quite touching kids with their hands. The corridor ahead was hot with lights.

"A big step, now. We got a blanket down. But you don't have to look."

Mary Dare took the giant step and several baby steps and found herself in the throbbing corridor. She paused, getting her bearings by herself. She was standing in the main hall to the school offices amidst bright lights and confusion and unfamiliar smears on the floor. To her left was the north hall, to her locker, and she turned automatically in that direction. Then she stopped, fascinated. Band music was seeping through the barred doors of the gynmasium at the far end of the north hall.

Hands turned her, started her in the other direction, hovered around her as though she might dissipate through their fingers like smoke. "This way. We're taking you into the study hall for now."

"*Study* hall!" moaned someone behind her in the line.

But news somehow was in the air, crackling in fragments.

"I guess for awhile they thought he was going to shoot up the *gym*."

"He's that kid that never comes to class. Somebody said they guessed he thought it was her fault he got a pink slip."

"Maybe he thought Mrs. Trask was her."

"Wonder what happened to Zeidel."

The patrolman heard that and answered. "Mr. Zeidel took a hit in the leg and, uh, one in the lower abdomen, and they're taking him by air ambulance to Great Falls. We think he heard the shots and ran up the hall and, uh, met the kid running out."

"Wonder if he got away," said Tom Barnes low in Mary Dare's ear, but the patrolman heard that, too.

"He ran out of the school and, uh, we don't have other information as yet."

Silenced, they filed through the double doors. Mary Dare took the first desk she came to; it wasn't where she usually sat. The others were taking desks at random around her, a small cluster in the huge hall. Through the west windows she could see the last red stain of daylight.

"Wonder how the game came out," somebody whispered.

Sounds in the room were getting back to normal. A desk lid creaked.

"In here, sir," said the patrolman at the door. Everyone looked up as a man in a dark suit and a tie came in and sat down on the corner of a desk opposite them. The man's eyes moved from face to face; he looked stricken at what he saw, but that too was beginning to seem normal.

"We won't be keeping you here long," he said. He nodded two or three times, promising. "Your parents are, most of them, the ones we got hold of or, uh, heard about it, are out there waiting. They're wanting to see you, and we won't be keeping you long, but there's just a few questions, just one or two—"

He paused, and his mouth worked rapidly. Was he going to cry? Mary Dare looked away just in time. The red stain in the windows was darkening into nightfall. It must be way past the time when the school buses left.

"Did any of you see him?"

They shook their heads. Somebody, Valier, jerked a furtive finger across his eyes.

A stray voice from the hall cut in, angry—"in the middle of Montana, for chrissake, shit like this ain't supposed to go on here—" and was cut off as the patrolman pulled the door closed.

"No."

"No."

"Mrs. Trask," said Tom Barnes. "We saw her keel over."

"Yes."

"Yes."

They all had seen that, they agreed, nodding. Ryan wore a slight smile. Tom Barnes was lazing back in his desk on his spine with one leg stuck out into the aisle and the other leg crossed over it. The teachers hated it when kids sat like that. As though in the white glare of a searchlight, Mary Dare saw the downy hair on the back of Tom's neck and the bleached blue flowers of his shirt and the fragile overwashed blue of his levis. He looked like love's fading dream, Mary Dare thought. She knew she must look worse.

The man in the dark suit massaged his eyes with his hands. Maybe they all really did look like fading dreams to him. "We know you saw that," he said. "And I'm so sorry. Please believe me. I'd give anything if you hadn't had to. But did you see him?" He was looking straight at Mary Dare.

"No," she said truthfully. "No."

He sighed and was silent. "All right," he said at last. "We might have to talk to some of you again. Just maybe. But we'll hope not. We'll hope he—"

His voice died away. They waited. Finally he sighed again and slid off the desk without explaining to them what it was he hoped for. "Anyway," he said, "I know some parents who are going to be awfully glad to see some kids."

"I wonder who won the game," said somebody else as they filed out of the study hall.

But that was one piece of news that hadn't floated down to them. Mary Dare thought the scrap of band music she had heard might have been the Libby Loggers' fight song, which might have meant Fort Maginnis was behind. She wondered if the kids had been scared to play basketball while policemen with shotguns guarded the exits of the gym, or if they had gotten used to it, or if they even had known about it.

In the adjacent classroom the faces of parents turned toward them like wet white blobs in overcoats and heavy jackets and snowy overshoes. "Oh shit," said Ryan, "the old man wouldn't—oh shit, he is here."

Mary Dare saw her mom and dad just before her mom grabbed her. She felt the crush of wool collar and a wet cheek in her neck.

"Told you she'd be all right," said her dad. He had on his good Stetson. Melted snow dripped from the brim.

Mary Dare's mother let her go, except for one tight handhold, and turned on Mary Dare's dad. "Can't you see?" she cried, picking up their argument. "She's my baby, she's fourteen, she's only fourteen, and now I'll never get her back."

"Linda," said Mary Dare's dad, and her mother stopped talking but went on crying quietly while her grip on Mary Dare's hand tightened.

"Hell, she's all right. These Montana kids grow up tough. You didn't see anything, did you, Mary Dare?"

"No," said Mary Dare. She barely could feel her fingers in her mother's grip.

They walked abreast through the double doors, her mother and father on either side of Mary Dare as though she might disappear in their hands. Someone brushed against them from behind, trying to get past the three of them in the archway; it was Tom Barnes, in a hurry, pulling on his satin team roping jacket as he went.

"You need a ride home, Tom?" called her father.
He glanced back. "No thanks, Doc. I got my truck."
"He's a good kid," said her dad. "Was he there too?"
"Yes," said Mary Dare.
Across the dark half-filled parking lot waited a school bus hung with painted banners, dieseling. Kids in Libby Logger letter jackets burst out of the double doors behind Mary Dare and her mother and father and ran yipping across the parking lot toward the bus.
"Pack of fools," said her dad angrily.
"No," said Mary Dare. "No, they're not."
You're the pack of fools, she wanted to say, but she shivered instead. In the refraction of frost under the exit lights she still could see the outline of Tom Barnes, hunching into his inadequate jacket against the freezing bite of the air and walking rapidly through the tumuli of shoveled snow toward the north lot. The sharp sounds of his boot heels on the scraped sidewalk receded as his shape faded beyond the radius of the lights, but for a moment Mary Dare followed him in her mind and faded with him into transparency in the dark. Far out in the circle of the mountains their glowing outlines fell to ash.

Runaway

There was nothing worse than a cowboy, and Carl was filthier than most. Kate spent all day cleaning his kitchen. She couldn't believe her eyes when she swept mummified flies out of the corners and fragments of bone out from under the table where he'd let the dog gnaw on them. Mouse droppings, even. And the walls were worse than the floor. Brown streaks where he'd spat his foul tobacco juice at the sink and missed. Other streaks, suspiciously yellow, where she knew he was using the sink as a urinal, being too lazy even to walk out the back door and aim at a bush. Muttering, she scoured the paint off the walls to get them clean.

Carl came home in the late afternoon and headed straight for the coffee pot on the back of the stove. Belatedly his eyes rose over the damp walls and paused on the clean bare windows.

"Aw, shit," he moaned.

"I tried to wash Mother's curtains," said Kate, "but they fell all to threads in the suds."

Carl had opened two or three cupboard doors, searching for the coffee mugs. At last he found one and peered inside it. "What did you do to these?"

"I scoured them out with bleach," Kate snapped. "Never saw such crud. And don't worry, I rinsed them, so it won't poison you. Unless you think it'll kill you to drink out of a clean cup."

Suddenly she felt so tired she didn't know if she could say another word without crying. She pulled out one of the scarred oak chairs and sat down at the kitchen table, feeling the slow ache settle into her shoulders.

Carl poured his coffee and walked over to the window. He studied the uncut grass in the yard and on the pasture hill as though he hoped to will a good soaking rain, or maybe straighten the bend in the road down to the mailboxes. Then he brought his cup and sat down across the table from her.

"Hell, Kate, it looks real good. Took me by surprise, is all."

She looked up eagerly. "Tomorrow I'll turn out the upstairs."

Carl blew on his coffee. "Kate, I sure wish you wouldn't do that. It'll just go back the way it was, the minute you leave."

Kate's throat felt raw. Fumes from the ammonia bottle, she told herself. She'd breathed ammonia fumes on her hands and knees today, and no thanks. Now she shut her eyes so she would not have to look at Carl, all grimed and grizzled as ever Father had been.

Through the tired blues and purples behind her stinging eyelids, starched curtains materialized at the windows and clean rugs unfolded on the freshly waxed floor. No. Might as well refinish that old pine floor, as long as she was imagining things, sand out all the scuffs and gouges and restain the boards. Sand and restain the woodwork, too. There was a place by the door that looked like the dog had chewed on it. Fresh paint on the walls. The kitchen was taking shape as Mother had kept it, or tried to keep it. Mother had had Father's filthy ways to fight, after all. And little enough help from Kate, if the truth were admitted.

"I just don't understand why you'd rather live dirty than clean," she said.

"Now look here," said Carl. "Where were you when I could have used some help?"

"Yes, throw that up to me."

He gulped coffee and glared at her. "Ain't like you have to hang around here and let it bother you. When are you going back to Kansas?"

"I hadn't made definite plans."

"You got a place to teach this fall? I'd think you'd want to be getting your applications out. Have to apply on your own nowadays, that right?"

"Yes. That's how we do it."

Carl breathed heavily through his nose and stared out the window, seeing whatever he saw. In the silence, Kate looked down at her hands, waterlogged and wrinkled from the futile day of scrubbing. An old housewife's hands. Like an echo of her own careful words to Mother Superior, the phrases planned carefully to elicit what she had to know—*my brother is recovering very well, they tell me a bypass is almost routine, but after all he is over fifty, and he needs someone to keep house for him. Maybe for the summer. I'll see him set straight and let you know*—her eyes on Mother Superior's face, her heart sinking at the relief she read there—*Kate, it may be just the thing—a chance for you to recover, too.*

She twisted her hands into her lap, hiding them. How she hated them. Blunt and liver-spotted, the hands of someone she never had planned to be.

"When do you *have* to be back?"

Kate looked up. "She didn't stipulate. It was just whenever—"

A terrible smell interrupted her, and she turned just in time to catch Carl's dog sneaking into the kitchen, his black and white coat dripping with muddy water and the odor of whatever carcass he had rolled in.

"Oh, not on my clean floor!" Kate wailed, too late, as the dog started to shake himself, found himself the center of attention, and dived under the table by Carl's feet.

Carl sprang up. "Christ! I've had all of this I can stomach. If I'd wanted a wife, I'd have married me one."

"But I worked all day!"

"It ain't your floor, Kate! It's been my floor for thirty years, and if I want that dog in here, I'm going to have him here!"

Carl stamped out, flinging the door behind him so hard that the dog, following but taking time to cast back a guilty look at Kate, nearly was caught in it and had to make a last-second dash for daylight.

Kate sat alone with the dying reverberations. She could think of no reason to move. Presently she heard the door of Carl's pickup slam and the motor fire into life. A moment later came the squeal of tires on gravel as he backed out on the road and tore away. She supposed he was going to town. Probably he would order himself a steak at the Empire, with no thought of cholesterol, and afterward drink beer with the regulars until he felt like coming home.

Her stomach had stirred at the thought of steak, and she

wondered if she was hungry. If she should eat something. A sandwich. Her mouth trembled.

The sun reddened in the west window, and the dog's puddles gradually dried in a pattern of transparent circles across the waxed floor. Several times Kate stirred at the sight of them, started to get up and wipe them away. But she stopped herself. Cleaning up after his dog at this point might seem submissive. It was difficult, though. Not doing it seemed rebellious. Which pose to take? The worst of it was, she could either clean the floor or leave it dirty, and either way Carl would come home and shrug. He didn't care, as long as she left him alone; his indifference made her one posture as meaningless as the other.

"So," she said aloud, without knowing what she meant.

She could not bear the thought of getting out Carl's loaf of white bread and peanut butter and making herself a sandwich to eat in solitude, so instead she wandered through the back door into the yard, where the grass grew knee high and smelled of summer. Her mother's lilacs still were alive by the gate, though crowded by the grass and grown to woody stems. She could see a few purple blooms, just turning to rust. Lilacs in June, how strange they would seem in Kansas. But here in the foothills of the Snowies, the season was short and the lilacs always bloomed late. Their perfume drew her, and the grass brushed against her legs as it had when she was twelve. Or eighteen. How strange that she could be eighteen one day, just starting out, full of promise, the brightest of all the St. Leo's girls; and, virtually the next day, be forty-eight and running out of choices.

She left the yard and its troubling perfume and crossed the road to where the few old pines cast the shade of warm needles over the sandstone ledge they had twisted through as seedlings and left riven and fissured. If she walked a little further, just beyond the lengthening claims of the shadows of the pines, she would be able to see as far as the row of mailboxes nailed to the plank on posts beside the main road into town.

Kate thought of fetching her suitcase and walking down the road with it. Maybe someone would offer her a lift to town, or even, say, as far as Billings. Let Carl come home and wonder what had happened to her. It would serve him right. She had enough money to stay in Billings. A few days, anyway. Hotel, meals—she visualized the fold of twenties in her wallet, saw herself laying down the last one beside some indifferent restaurant cashier.

What did they do with people who ran out of money? She knew the answer, of course, in a general way, but to think about the reality of stepping over the line that separated women like her from women in shelters made her feel sicker than the idea of eating Carl's bread and peanut butter did.

She wondered what they would do with her if she went back to Kansas. She couldn't be the first failure they'd had on their hands; probably they had a statute. Her health was good. If she couldn't find another teaching position, maybe they'd set her to scrubbing.

Kate turned and walked uphill, away from the shadow of her thoughts. Above the house, the road dwindled into two dusty tracks where only Carl's pickup kept the grass from closing over the old ruts. Soon she had to watch her footing. She stepped on a hummock that seemed solid and felt herself slide a foot or more through sharp bearded grasses into the bottom of a rut. Her ankle throbbed from the unexpected wrench, and for a step or two she limped.

It had been an old wagon road, that was why the ruts were so deep. Teams of horses had struggled and fought their way uphill a foot at a time while men had cursed and lashed at them and wheels of iron and hardwood had dug deeper and deeper into churning mud. Kate shuddered.

The road had led up to the old Ballard place and from there into the real Snowies. Father had liked to tell how, as a boy, he had helped Grandfather and old Fred Fergusson and Des Ballard snake fir poles for the corrals down from the mountains along that road. It had been a way he could think of himself as part of the Fergusson and Ballard legend, although at its very end.

The corrals appeared to be as run down as the rest of the ranch. The big arena, where Father often had held up to two hundred head of horses, was overgrown with dock and bindweed and had collapsed at the lower end, the rotten poles tented over an un-thwarted new growth of hawthornes. Apparently Carl still was using the round corral and the loading chute. She could see where new posts had been set, and where new sawed boards had replaced some of the old logs on the loading ramp.

At the door of the barn she stopped. Shingles had fallen from the roof, and the famous sixteen-foot log lintel sagged lower than her head. Underfoot the ground was mounded up from years of horses' hoofs and the accumulated layers of pulverized manure. She would have to bend almost double to walk inside. Was it safe? A thousand memories called her, a thousand warned her off. How many long-dead horses had walked through this cavernous door into sunlight, jingling in harness or saddled for a day's work or under halter for another trader to look over? How many horses had had to empty their bowels to build up the mound under her feet, dried and flaky now in a texture like tinder? She could hear the squeal of a horse, her father's shout, and the blows—an oak spoke from a wagon wheel, again and again—*kick me, will you, you son of a bitch*—the sound of hardwood socking into flesh, the sound her mother had lived with.

It was a great country for men and dogs, someone had written, but hell on women and horses. Kate as a high school senior, coming upon that sentence in the assigned reading for her Montana history class, had recognized at once what it meant, hearing in it the sound of a blow; and that was the reason why, taking a vow of poverty a year later, she had not had the slightest qualm about renouncing either her claim to the ranch or to its legend.

Now she looked at herself more coldly. What if she had been tougher? Less ready to run away from one prescribed way of living into another?

It was as that moment—like an answer to her question, she thought at the time—that she was drawn out of her self-absorption by a glimpse of movement, a stir of life from the round corral.

Kate went to investigate, picking a way through the rampant growth of weeds, walking over stunted wild roses that raked her ankles. She climbed as she had as a child on corral poles rubbed to velvet by years of weather and the backs of horses, half noticing the coarse black hairs caught on a splinter, left by some long forgotten horse of Father's from a time when horsehair caught on a corral fence was ordinary, unnoticeable. There in the middle of the corral, foreleg raised as though in preamble to what was coming next, ears pricked with interest in Kate, was a small bay mare.

Kate sat on a sandstone boulder in the midday sun, greasing harness. The harness had been hanging in the barn so long that the leather was cracked and the metal parts were rigid with the residual grime of the years. Nothing about it recalled the living tissue from which it had been cut, and she didn't suppose it ever would be supple again. She hadn't even been able to find real harness grease, and the boot grease she was using soaked into her hands faster than it did the leather. But she kept dipping into the can with her fingers, rubbing in the gobs of grease, breathing its pungency, while dark lines grew under her fingernails and around her knuckles. Everything was as it always had been. The sun bore down on her back, and the air smelled of turpentine. Grasshoppers snapped and bounded in the weeds.

"Picked her up at a sale at Grass Range," Carl had answered when she asked him about the bay mare. "Thought I could ride her a few times and sell her again for gentle broke, make a few dollars on her, but hell, she's spoiled. She knows every trick. I'm going to haul her into the yards in town next week, get what I can out of her. She ain't worth keeping in a corral and feeding hay to."

"She reminds me of a mare Father broke one summer."

He glared at her, and she recognized her brother's blue eyes as clear as ever in the webbed and sagging face. "Since when were you interested in Father's horses, Kate? I thought you—what do they call it?—renounced all that."

"I renounced the property. That doesn't mean I can't be interested."

"You renounced the ranch, remember? And then off you went, so smart."

Kate opened her mouth to remind him that they were all each other had left, but it was too late.

"I suppose it looks better to you now. Worth something, now I've busted my ass over it. Now that I've seen Mother and Father

193

through, all by myself. Oh, shit, don't start to cry about it."

"She's so pretty. That's the only reason I asked about her."

"Don't you try to ride her, Kate! She'll break your neck. All in hell she knows is get the bit in her teeth and run with it. She ain't never going to be no good, so don't you get any ideas."

"Oh, I won't!" Kate had promised, silently adding the qualifier, *try to ride her*.

Now she rubbed boot grease into the old single harness and smiled to herself. Carl wasn't the only one of his children Father ever taught to handle a horse. Those last two summers on the ranch, before she finished high school, and while Carl was off on the circuit more often than he was home, getting his bones pounded permanently back into his sockets by the saddle broncs, Kate had been the one Father turned to.

Why had Father, in the middle years of the nineteen-fifties, spent two summers breaking horses to harness? At the time, it hadn't occurred to Kate to ask questions; what Father did, he did. But now, as she speculated about his reasons, they became more and more elusive. Nostalgia, perhaps? Father would have seemed the last man to be moved by sentiment, but finally Kate could think of no better explanation that than, somehow, during those summers he had been reliving his crucial years. The horses he was breaking to work had no value, after all. Kate had no idea what he finally had done with them; nobody would have wanted to buy them. By the nineteen-fifties, farming with horses virtually was a thing of the past ("Thank God," her mother had said, "and let them beat on the machinery if they feel like it,") and the popularity of pleasure harness clubs still was years in the future.

Most of what she knew about Father, Kate now realized, she had learned during those long afternoons of dust and sunburn, jogging up and down the road behind a skin-kneed, trembling, part-Percheron bronc with the bridle lines in her hands, while Father followed, holding the rope attached to the W and reminiscing about the dark drought years of the thirties when he'd managed to save a little haycrop and survive the winters by breaking the neighbors' colts to work in exchange for the use of them.

The thirties had been his years. He had been almost famous, a legend of a man when it came to handling teams of horses. Hardly a work team in the country, there during the thirties, that Father hadn't started. He remembered them all, which ones like this bay mare he'd broken of stampeding, which of baulking, which ones he'd lost in the sleeping sickness epidemic; and he described them all to Kate while he passed on to her the lore of generations. How to feel a mouth through the lines, how to rig a W. What the old wagon bosses had known about handling teams, what they'd learned from the teamsters through the ages, what the ancient Romans must have known about handling chariot horses. All that hard-won, esoteric, treasured lore, all doomed to be forgotten with the end of the horse age. That Father might have passed it on to her those summers only because Carl was off rodeoing was a suspicion Kate had refused to let surface.

Now Kate dropped the empty can of boot grease into the weeds and stood up with her arms full of unwilling loops and stiffened whorls of leather.

"Hello, pretty girl," she said, and the bay mare raised her head in recognition, her white forehead star a beacon.

She was halterbroken. Twice, picking afternoons when Kate was certain Carl had gone to town for the rest of the day, probably to hole up at the Empire and play cards, she had been in the corral with the mare and had led her around and picked up her feet. Kate thought it possible that, having been started under saddle, the mare might spook at the sight of someone controlling her lines from behind her, but Kate was sure she could handle her. Plenty of women drove horses. Cowgirls, hands, daughters of men like Father, women like the one Kate might have become, women who did all the work on ranches and broke horses and wore their blue jeans faded and low.

It was worth a try. Let Carl see for himself what a hand she could make.

Kate let herself and her unwieldly bundle through the gate into the corral, and the mare threw back her head and snorted at the shape and smell, breathing rollers through her nose, her haunches gathered.

"Come now, come now," Kate chided, offering her palmful of oats.

The insistent tickle of lips on her palm, sending the sensations up her arms, dissolving in her shoulders, woke recollections of a body she had forgotten. She felt the weight of the sun on her cropped hair. Her muscles had gone slack. She breathed deep in pine scented air and dust and the sweet gaseous smell of the horse, and her nipples woke and remembered themselves and contracted.

She might have been eighteen again, blood and bone. Even her clothes were the same she had worn those other summers, the very same, the clean if stale and long-folded shirt and levis and pair of boots dug out of the box in Mother's old room. The mare flicked away a fly with a swish of her black tail, as unconscious and easy as horses through the ages always had switched at flies, and turned and sank her teeth through the fragile cloth into Kate's forearm.

Kate felt the jolt in her shoulder as her fist smacked against the mare's forehead before the vulnerable flesh of her eighteen-year-old self felt the pain of the bite. The mare jerked back against the halter rope, snorting spume, and Kate hit her again with the side of her hand in the soft part of her nose.

"You bitch!" she shouted.

The remains of her sleeve hung in wet flaps. The sad bleached cloth, last washed and ironed and folded away by Mother, had dis-integrated more than been torn away by the circle of teeth. Tears sprang as she tried to examine the wound.

"Bitch!" she cried again, out of the pain of betrayal. In the wake of her own voice she heard those other words of hers, breaking over a room finally silenced, the eighth-grade girls petrified in their seats, finally seeing her, Kate, really seeing her for the first time as their eyes whitened with a new understanding of fear. *You little bitches! Make fun of me, will you?*

"I thought I loved you!" Kate sobbed at the mare. Getting a short hold on the halter rope, she reached back for the load of har-ness and heaved it up. Straps and buckles bounced over the mare's back, settling into place in a brief puff of dust except for the awkward protruberances and angles as deformed as rictus where the leather had refused to soften. The mare was trying to rear, trying to dance or flinch or shrink out from under such a strange creaking burden, but Kate had her snubbed short now. Kate was ready when the foreleg shot out in a strike, and she felt the thrill of her boot on bone when she kicked back.

"So you think you know it all!" she shouted.

The mare, lathered and cringing, was watching her just as the girls had watched her for that one moment before the voices from the corridor broke in—*It's Sister Kathryn, she's screaming and swearing at us, we don't know what's wrong*!

"Oh, I'm going to drive you now!" promised Kate.

She had wondered if she would remember how to buckle the harness, but her hands snapped and looped up the traces and fastened the crupper on their own while her eyes guarded against the sudden subversive movement of the neck or the snaking foreleg. Her hands slid the snaffle bit over the mare's tongue, the split headstall over the ears and poll. The mare champed at the bit, foam staining to pink from the rust.

Kate snapped the lines to the headstall and fell back and slapped them over the mare's back. The mare took one or two hesitant, stiff-legged steps. Then she was crossing the corral at a hard walk, while Kate, walking behind her with the lines wrapped around her hands, felt the familiar jolt in her shoulders, the charge of energy. Here we come! There should be a celebration! Bands playing, flags flying, a crowd cheering from the opposite side of a dusty arena. Carl should see us now!

"Do you know how to back up?"

Drooling pink, the mare shook her head at the pressure of the lines. Like any bronc that had been started under saddle, she expected a weight on her back, pressure on her neck. The blinkers on the bridle kept her from looking back at the strange source of control. She fought the bit, stretching her neck and lifting her nose skyward in her attempt to see behind her. Kate sawed at the lines, forcing her back one tentative step, then another.

"I believe I can back you up to the wagon," she said aloud.

Earlier in the day she had shifted stacks of junk and tugged and heaved and finally managed to roll the light wagon out of the shed, where Carl apparently had stored it with the debris and relics of a world gone by, and pushed it ground level beside the corral. It sat there now. Kate knew by rights she should drive the mare on foot for a few days, let her get used to the lines, but too much time already had passed. She couldn't wait.

"Don't you bite me again, bitch," she said. She wished she knew more obscenities, but Father and even Carl always had guarded their potent words from the womenfolk. She wished she had not closed her ears so reflexively on the whispers of the eighth-grade girls. She wound up the lines and ran her hand down one black foreleg, then the other, buckling the straps of the W and passing the rope through them. Then she swung the corral gate open, stepped back in a fumble of lines and rope, and shouted at the mare.

Daylight widened in the gate, with a clear view of the road down through the sandstone ledges, the tops of pines and the shingles of the house, the glint of Castle Creek and the hills rising out of the hay meadows on the other side of the highway. The mare pawed. Kate could feel the tingle through the lines, feel the mare's urge to run for it. The first trace of doubt clouded her own excitement. Here was Kate, plunging in as usual where she wasn't wanted, trying to do too much too soon. What would Father say?

But Father was in his grave, and Kate for once was on her own. She got a good footing with her bootheels in the gritty mountain topsoil and braced herself to saw and shout the mare into position in front of the wagon.

"All right," she said at last. From the spring seat she could see over the mare's back and as far down the road as the mailboxes. The air smelled thin and clean; she felt light-headed from it. The lines were wrapped around her hands, the end of the rope was secure in her armpit. All her joints ached from being jerked along from boothold to boothold by the lines, but her legs in the faded old levis felt as stout as trees when she braced them against the silvered footboard. She breathed out and released the wagon brake.

A pause. The mare tested the drag on the traces, reared, reared again against the puzzling counterweight that held her back. Then she hurled herself against it. The wheels creaked in a quarter-turn through summer grass, and Kate threw herself back against the lines, but too late, when she felt the mare fumble the bit on her tongue and catch it between her teeth. Kate shot forward, then backward on the seat. The wheels skidded across sandstone, bounced over the ruts, and landed. Kate grabbed for the seat and hung on. She still was being jerked forward by the left line, but her end of the right line was limp. The other end, two or three feet of it, whipped and cracked from the mare's jaw where, leaning into the bit as she would have under saddle, she had clenched her teeth.

The barn shot by in a series of crazy bounds. They were headed downhill over sand, gravel, long grass. Kate tried hauling on the left line, but it was like trying to pull a limb off a tree, and she needed the hand to hold on with. The mare's ears were flattened, her breath roared through her clenched teeth. Kate's eyes streamed with wind. There went the house, windows as empty as astonishment. Kate hung on. They were surviving the bend in the road on two wheels. Then one wheel hit a rock and catapulted over it. No time to think about being thrown out of the wagon, they were bearing down the the mailboxes now. Then the clatter of hoofs and wheels on asphalt, and a screech of wrath—of gears—and Kate looked up to see the red truck with its front wheels skewed into the ditch and Carl's face and the dog's face paralyzed in the windshield.

They were on the highway, they were going to be killed—but no, nothing would stop the mare now. The wagon bucked across the asphalt behind her, bucked down the borrow pit and up the other side. Strands of wire sprang apart with a scream of burst staples. Trees, rocks, grass and sky blurred together into a running stream of time that had caught Kate and was tumbling her headlong toward the end. She understood her life now. Her new beginning had been illusory. She had run, and run, always supposing she was running from something, when in fact she was hurtling toward something. Had Father known? Had he been trying to warn her, those summers with the horses? She herself had no chance to cry out a warning; the wind would have torn it away even if she could have found words for the indifferent little girls. She, and the mare too, were roaring at top speed through a dangerous landscape until, very soon now, they would crash and both their necks would be broken. They had crested the hill; they never would survive the downward plunge.

Something chafed at her armpit. At first she could not remember why she had kept the rope. But, yes. It had a purpose. She even remembered what it was.

Kate braced herself against the footboard and got hold of the rope in both hands and threw her weight against it.

What she saw, as the rope closed its W-shaped rigging through the mare's breastcollar and the straps on her forelegs, was not the sudden choke on those striving front hoofs, but, instead, the mare's hindquarters rising into her face and rising higher, the black tail flourishing like a flag against the blue, in the endless moment before the mare completed her somersault in a tangle of harness.

Taking control, Kate realized with irritation, potentially was even riskier than not taking control. She watched as the wagon sailed over the thrashing mare, came down with a banshee howl of splintering wood, bounced back up into the air as deliberately as if it were doing it on purpose, and landed again with finality, upside down. All four wheels went on turning, while dust and pine needles floated back down to earth through shafts of late sunlight.

The mare kicked free of the last trace and heaved herself over on her belly. She got her forelegs out in front of her, gathering herself for the try for her feet. Pine needles hung in her mane.

Kate flexed her fingers. Her face felt raw, but most of the pain seemed located in her ribs. She could feel her toes. If she had known she was so durable, how much more she might have tried! The question now was how to get out of this wedge between pine tree and boulder where she seemed to have landed. She could not remember when she had parted from the wagon seat.

She tried turning her head. The hill fell away below her. She could see the track she had cut, all the way down to the meadows, and a speck of red, headed her way in a silent frenzy of purpose. It was Carl's red pickup. It charged through the fence without stopping for the gate and split the creek in two equal sprays. As it ripped through the meadows and commenced the hill climb, she began to hear its engine noise, faint at first, like an angry insect in four wheel drive.

Carl was headed for her by the shortest route. For reconciliation? Kate could only hope. She gathered herself, crying a little as the raw flesh of her arms scraped against pine bark, for the heave out of the wedge to meet Carl on her feet.

About the Author

Mary Clearman Blew grew up on a ranch in Montana, on the site of her great-grandfather's original homestead, and attended the University of Montana and the University of Missouri. She teaches fiction writing and literature at Lewis-Clark State College in Lewiston, Idaho.